Just My Imagination

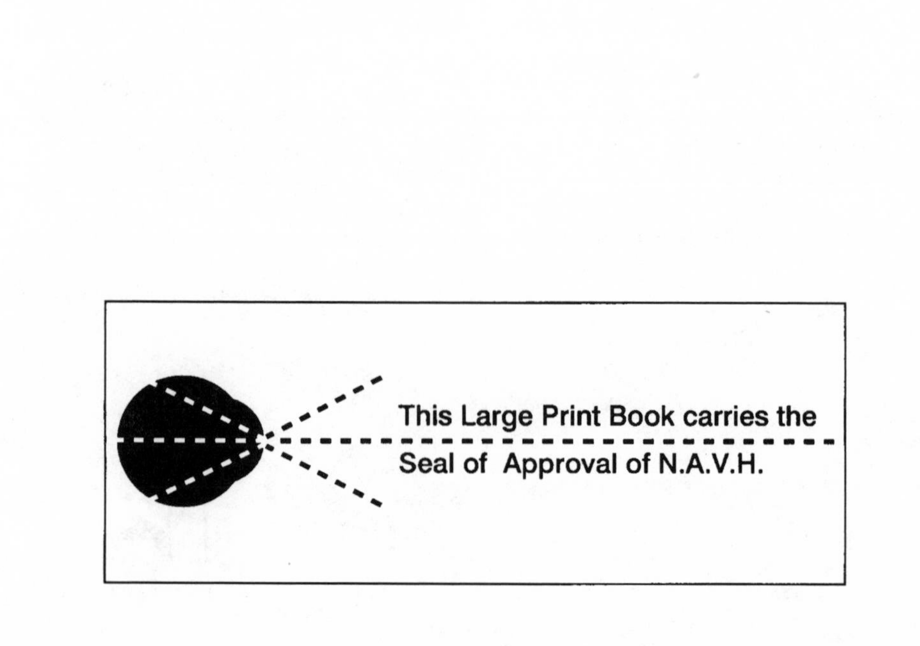
This Large Print Book carries the
Seal of Approval of N.A.V.H.

Just My Imagination

Karen Sandler

Thorndike Press • Waterville, Maine

Published in 2002 by arrangement with Karen Sandler.

Thorndike Press Large Print Romance Series.

The tree indicium is a trademark of Thorndike Press.

The text of this Large Print edition is unabridged.
Other aspects of the book may vary from the original edition.

Cover design by Deirdre Wait.

Set in 16 pt. Plantin by Myrna S. Raven.

Printed in the United States on permanent paper.

ISBN 0-7862-4524-7 (lg. print: hc : alk. paper)

To my mom, who never stopped believing in me. I love you, Mom!

Chapter 1

Face set in concentration, Steve Walker plunged his hand a second time into the murky depths of his daughter's backpack. As Corazon regarded him with her dark eyes, Steve probed past fruit-snack wrappers and pencil stubs, fingers finally coming to rest against a soft, sticky lump.

He dislodged the gooey mess and held it out to his almost seven-year-old daughter. "What might this be?"

"Might be peana' butter 'n' jelly." She leaned closer, sniffed delicately. "Starbaby jelly."

How many days ago had that particular sandwich taken up residence in the bottom of her backpack? With trepidation, he reached back into the black hole. His always fertile imagination conjured up an animated fantasy of first his arm, then his entire body being sucked into the bottomless pit.

His mouth widened into a slow grin. Real potential here for his next computer game — *Backpack Abyss*. Hapless parents battling roving globs of bread and peanut butter, skewered by pencil stubs.

Finally his wandering fingers found what they were looking for. He pinched the edge of the crumpled piece of paper and pulled it free. He held it out to Corazon's earnest face.

"When did Mr. Harper give you this note?" He tried to be stern, but he really wanted to grip her in a tight hug, and feel her thin brown arms wrap trustingly around his shoulders.

She shrugged, the motion a near exact imitation of his own. He brimmed with parental pride, marveling at how quickly she'd adapted in the eighteen months she'd been his.

With an effort, he returned to the matter at hand. "Your teacher wanted you to give this to me right away."

She nodded solemnly. "Yes, Daddy."

He laid the jelly-smeared sheet on the kitchen counter and picked up a damp rag. "Principal Tipton is probably pretty angry at Daddy for ignoring this note."

"Ms. Tipton is always mad anyway," Corazon said.

As Steve wiped the note clean, he had to agree. He'd never met the woman, only spoken with her on the phone after each of Corazon's playful pranks. The Jell-O in the water fountain, the corn snake in the teacher's desk drawer . . . Okay, the haircut she'd given her friend Jenny would take a while to grow out, especially the spot Cora had colored with permanent marker . . .

But what he saw as high spirits and harmless experimentation, Ms. Tipton insisted were signs of budding juvenile delinquency. The woman had no sense of humor. In fact, after a half dozen rancorous phone calls with her, he was convinced she had snakes instead of hair.

Now there was an idea for a game — *Gorgon Schoolmistress.* He could program each writhing snake on the Gorgon's head with a different venom, and the hero would have to find the right shields to protect himself. Maybe Ms. Gor— Ms. Tipton would agree to model for the animator.

When he'd swiped enough strawberry jelly off the paper, he read the appointment time penned neatly on the note. She'd expected him at the school at three o'clock. An hour and a half ago. Principal Tipton would truly be in a fury.

"Daddy!" Corazon gasped, pulling his attention from the note. She stared in fascinated horror out the front window. "She's here!"

Steve moved up behind his daughter, settling his hands on her shoulders. "Who's here?" He squinted through the cut glass of the window, glimpsing the lines of a severe navy suit. The face above the suit shifted and fractured Picasso-like through the ornate glass window.

Corazon craned her neck up at him, excitement bursting in her dark eyes. "Ms. Tipton!"

A sharp tip-tap of steps on the porch, then the doorbell rang. "Daddy, what're we gonna do?"

Even the doorbell sounded angry as it trilled a second time. "We let her in, *mija*," he answered, using the Spanish endearment to reassure her. As he went to the door, he felt his daughter wrapping her arms around his legs.

"Tell her our dog ate the note, Daddy."

"But we don't have a dog, *mija.* Cousin Denny is allergic to animals."

She gripped him tighter. "Then a time-morpher took it. Came out of the 'puter and gobbled it up."

"I don't think Ms. Tipton believes in time-morphers."

"What're we gonna do?" Corazon said again as her arms cut off the circulation in his legs.

"I'll think of something, *mija*," he soothed as he gripped the doorknob.

By the time he opened the door, he'd come up with several creative excuses, each sillier than the last. But it turned out not to have mattered. Because when he saw her on his doorstep — her slim legs set off by navy spiked heels, the dangerous curves at hip and waist, the sleek black hair framing a delicate heart-shaped face — all coherent thought fled.

As a tantalizing scrap of red — *red!* — lace peeked from the edge of her skirt, he realized he was wrong about one thing. Ms. Tipton was no Gorgon. But he was absolutely right about another — she was blazing, spitting mad.

Katherine Elizabeth Tipton considered herself a reasonable, levelheaded woman. As principal of Gardenview Elementary in California's Sierra foothills, she supervised a staff of thirty. She monitored the progress of 451 K-through-sixth-grade students. She eked out of a constantly shrinking budget sufficient funds both for educating her students and maintaining aging school buildings. She possessed not only administrative credentials and a Master's in Education, but an MBA as well.

Yet with every phone call to Mr. Steven Walker, Katherine's cool, calm demeanor dissolved into uncontrolled annoyance.

He didn't seem to intend to annoy her. In fact, she couldn't quite put a finger on what he did that set her off. It wasn't the fact that he was a flake, although she'd never understood how the State of California could have approved such a goofball as an adoptive parent. A single parent at that.

And it wasn't that he was neglectful of his daughter's academic performance. Cora's teacher from last year said that Mr. Walker had attended every parent event — conferences, PTA meetings, back-to-school night — he'd even volunteered in the classroom every other week.

It was just that with each phone call, she became more and more convinced that the man simply had no clue as to the gravity of his daughter's misbehavior. Nothing Cora did seemed worth taking seriously. *She's only expressing herself,* Mr. Walker would say in response to every incident involving Cora.

Katherine headed up the walk of Mr. Walker's narrow, three-story Victorian, her all-business high heels clicking on the walk. The late-afternoon October sunlight glanced off the peach and pale coral adorning the neat clapboards and gingerbread trim. The wraparound front porch wore a darker shade of coral, each post in the balustrade impeccably painted.

She felt a stab of envy at the sight of the well-kept house. She couldn't help comparing the perfection of Mr. Walker's Victorian with the tumbledown state of her own handyman's special. Not that her house couldn't outshine this one someday, when she finally completed its renovation. If she ever did complete it. Her overbearing mother was supervising the work and driving her and the contractors crazy. They were starting work on the ancient plumbing today and all of a sudden her mother was an expert on pipes . . .

With an effort, she pushed her irritation aside and refocused her energy on the problem at hand — Mr. Walker. Mounting the porch steps, she straightened her navy blue suit, tugging at her skirt to conceal the red lace slip she'd pulled on this morning with guilty pleasure. Jaw set, she stabbed at the doorbell with her finger.

She heard movement inside the house, shuffling feet and furiously whispered voices, one of them clearly Mr. Walker's. She caught a quick impression of someone peering out the cut-glass front window. Expecting the imminent opening of the door, she squared her shoulders.

The door did not open. She heard the whispering again, the heavy scraping of a foot as if something weighted down the leg attached to it. She jabbed the doorbell again. Still no response.

Worked into a self-righteous fury, she organized in her mind all the cutting things she intended to say to Steve Walker. Determined, she raised her finger for a third poke at the doorbell.

The door opened suddenly and she stopped her hand in midair. The sight of Steve Walker's chest, broad and flat and six inches from her nose, stopped her mind in mid-thought.

Restarting her brain, Katherine tipped her head up to meet Mr. Walker's eyes. She blinked at their coppery warmth, narrowed her own suspiciously at the slow smile that spread across his face. She clenched her jaw to keep her own face from softening in response.

His grin broadened, as if he'd detected her reaction. She diverted her eyes from his smile, her restless gaze taking in the soft brown waves of his hair, the strong column of his neck, the wide shoulders flexing in forest green plaid flannel. She had to squelch an unexpected urge to put her hands on those shoulders and slide them slowly along the musculature, to lock behind his neck and —

"Ms. Tipton?" he asked, the curiosity clear in his face.

A flush rose in her cheeks as she batted down her fantasy. *Stop panting after this man,* she scolded herself. *You are nearly engaged.* But somehow she couldn't bring her fiancé's face to mind. Alan didn't hold a candle to this man.

"Mr. Walker," she said a little breathlessly, then added a needed sternness to her voice. "You seem to have forgotten our appointment."

"Please call me Steve." He stepped aside, gesturing her past him into the house. "I'm sorry, but I'm afraid Cora's backpack ate your note."

She eyed him sharply as she squeezed past him, not liking the close proximity the doorway forced them into. Once she was on a level with him she could see he was only a few inches taller than her five-foot-seven. Holding him in her arms, she reflected, would be an easy, comfortable gesture. She put distance between them as soon as she was inside.

Steve shut the door, then moved penguin-like toward the living room. For the first time, she noticed Corazon clinging to the backs of his legs. Katherine might have smiled at his awkward walk if she hadn't been so intent on keeping her expression serious.

"Come sit," he said, grabbing up an armload of magazines from the plum-colored leather sofa.

Just as Katherine began to sit on the plump cushions, an explosion of sound shook the house. Startled, Katherine stumbled backwards onto the sofa in an awkward sprawl.

She tugged down on her navy skirt frantically, covering the hem of her slip. "What was that?"

"Cousin Denny," Mr. Walker answered placidly, as he peeled his daughter from his legs.

He settled in a matching plum armchair set at a right angle to the sofa and pulled his daughter into his lap. As he shifted to accommodate Corazon, his denim-clad knees brushed against Katherine's.

She pulled primly away and scanned the warm, comfortable room. She had to admire the spill of lace curtains at the windows, the riotous cabbage-rose wallpaper and satiny cherrywood molding.

Her gaze finally rested on the magazines on the sturdy oak side table. Each cover sported lurid graphics from various electronic games. She recognized the magazine titles — she'd confiscated enough of them from her fifth- and sixth-grade students.

Katherine wrinkled her nose in distaste. "Cora likes video games?"

Corazon kept her wary eyes on Katherine. "Those are Daddy's."

Her father grinned apologetically. "I forgot to take them back upstairs. I was looking for the ice-world defense against the fooma bugs."

Another bang rattled through the house, and this time Katherine pinpointed its source as somewhere upstairs. "What *is* that?" Katherine asked again.

"Cousin Denny," Cora said solemnly. "He's 'sperimenting."

"*Ex*perimenting," Mr. Walker said absently as he dug through the stack of magazines. He plucked one from the pile. "This is a great issue."

A crash and a clatter shuddered through the ceiling, and Katherine peered apprehensively heavenward. When she turned back to Mr. Walker, she came face-to-face with a ten-legged purple bug with a face like a crazed bunny.

She nudged the magazine he held out for her back from her nose. "Very nice."

He turned the magazine back to peruse the cover fondly. "I love computer games. The colors, the sounds. The way a talented software designer can make graphics come alive."

A childlike delight suffused his face, and the warmth in his coppery eyes started a glow in the vicinity of Katherine's heart. She had a sudden, inexplicable desire to sit with him at a computer, a mouse in her hand, blasting fooma bugs out of the ice world.

She slammed a lid on that crazy notion. "I'm here to discuss Corazon." An attenuated boom issued from above; this time Katherine barely flinched. "We have some definite concerns about her behavior."

The child in question scrunched even farther into her father's lap, her hands in a near death grip around his neck. The loud noises from upstairs might not have frightened her, but Katherine's words certainly did.

"In the" — Mr. Walker untwined Cora's fingers — "in the classroom?"

"Partly, Mr. Walker —"

"Call me Steve, please."

"Steve," she acquiesced. Then his warm smile must have shaken something loose in her brain, because she added, "I'm Katherine." She snapped her mouth shut. She had never invited any parent to use her first name.

"Katherine." He rolled her name across his tongue as if it were a particularly luscious chocolate.

A shiver traveled down Katherine's spine as he gazed at her expectantly. What had she been about to say?

She forced her mind back into gear. "Are you aware that Cora has been holding screaming contests at school?"

"Corazon Estrella Walker!" There was only mild censure in his tone. "Have you been screaming in the classroom?"

Cora gazed up at him sweetly. "No, Daddy. Only out on the playground."

Steve turned his focus to Katherine. "She can't scream on the playground?"

"It's against school rules," Katherine informed him.

His brows arched up in surprise. "Children aren't allowed to scream at school?"

"Of course not," she said, feeling defensive. "If all the children screamed out on the yard —"

He fixed his eyes on hers. "Do all the children scream?"

"No —" A series of firecracker pops seemed to dance on the ceiling. Katherine waited until the room had quieted again. "Only the small group led by Cora."

His face relaxed again into a smile. "Then I don't see the problem."

"But, Mr. Walker — Steve," she amended, jumping a little as one last pop hurried to join its brothers. "When teachers hear a child scream, they're immediately concerned that a student has been hurt and —"

"You're right," he said, turning a dazzling smile on Katherine. "I hadn't thought of it that way."

His capitulation, not to mention his smile, confused Katherine. "You can see how it might frighten the teachers."

"Of course. I agree." He looked down at his daughter. "Okay, *mija.* All future screaming contests should be held at home."

Cora peered up at him earnestly. "Okay, Daddy. Can I go watch Cousin Denny?"

"Sure." Cora squirmed down from his lap and disappeared upstairs.

Steve leaned back, draping his arms across the back of the leather armchair. "Problem solved."

Katherine could only stare, open-mouthed. "But nothing's solved!"

"Cora will keep her word."

"Perhaps on that issue — but this isn't just about the screaming." Katherine scooted to the edge of the sofa, intent on making her point. "Now about the Jell-O in the water fountain —"

He waved a negligent hand. "She just wanted to see if it would turn the water red."

"But it clogged the drain!"

"And I paid the plumbing bill. Which Cora's repaying me from her allowance."

Katherine leaned forward, only half-aware that her knees were perilously near his again. "The snake in Mr. Harper's desk —"

"She only meant to show it to him." He propped his elbows on his knees, his face millimeters from hers. "Cora didn't know he was so frightened of snakes."

She felt the warmth of his breath as he spoke, and sensed the heat in his molten-copper eyes. Her gaze stopped on his mouth and traced the line of his lips with fascination.

"So you see," he said, and she followed the intriguing movement, "there's no problem."

Somehow, she couldn't find fault with his logic. "But what about the pictures?"

His gaze dipped down to her knees. "Pictures?"

She looked down automatically to see what drew his attention. A two-inch section of crimson lace and satin peeked from the edge of her skirt. In a mortified rush, her good sense returned, and she scrambled back from him. She slid halfway down the sofa's length to put an extra measure of distance between them.

"Cora draws pictures," Katherine stated, concealing her slip again with sharp tugs, "of monsters, alien creatures, strange worlds. The school psychologist is quite concerned."

Steve broke into an entirely unexpected burst of laughter. "Those are just video-game characters."

Katherine crossed her arms across her chest to ward off his good humor. "It still doesn't seem quite healthy for a little girl like Cora."

"But she's got some great ideas." He rose from his chair, holding out a hand to her. "Come on upstairs, I'll show you."

No way would she take that hand. No possible way would she go upstairs with him, where the mysterious Cousin Denny was obviously concocting pipe bombs.

Suddenly, thunderous footsteps on the front porch put the entire scene into pause mode.

The front door banged open with an energy that seemed capable of blasting it from its hinges. Just as Katherine snatched her hand back, twin teenage girls, in a clamor of excitement and high-pitched voices, made their flamboyant entrance.

"Uncle Steve!" one of them squealed, although which of the redheaded girls had spoken Katherine couldn't tell. They hugged him in turn, as if they hadn't seen him in years, with all the enthusiasm of fourteen-year-olds.

The girls slammed the door shut again, then slung backpacks in quick succession under a table. "We won!" said one twin.

"First place!" her sister said, tossing back her long fall of red hair.

"We're going to the finals!" the first said, feet prancing in an exuberant jig.

Steve gave them each another hug. "Fantastic!" He backed away and turned to Katherine. "Melinda, Theresa, this is Ms. Tipton. These are my nieces. They live with me when their parents are on the road."

Katherine rose, and the girls gravely shook her hand in turn. Spying their white-cotton gloves, Katherine asked, "You're cheerleaders?"

"Ewww," they squealed in unison, their pretty freckled faces screwed up in disgust. "Yuk."

Steve laughed. "Melinda and Theresa perform synchronized traffic direction."

"Synchronized . . ." Katherine's questioning voice trailed off as she took in the khaki-trimmed-with-red camp shirts and shorts the girls wore. Neatly lettered plastic name tags were pinned to their pocket flaps, and whistles dangled around their necks.

"They're top of their division," Steve continued proudly. "If they win the state finals, they go on to the Nationals."

The girls cheered at the top of their lungs, rivaling Cousin Denny's noise production, while Steve pumped his arm triumphantly.

"Do you want to see?" Melinda asked Katherine.

As Katherine scrambled for a response, Theresa asked Steve, "Which one should we show her?"

He squeezed Theresa's shoulder. "I'm partial to the Flooded Intersection routine, myself."

"Four Lanes Become One," the girls

chimed, jumping up and down.

"You'll love this," Steve said to Katherine, steering her back to the sofa. "You have the tape?" he asked Theresa.

She looked up from her backpack and flourished a cassette. "Right here."

Steve popped the tape into a nearby boom box while the girls positioned themselves side by side, one slightly behind the other. When he saw they were ready, he pushed the play button and hurried back to sit beside Katherine.

John Philip Sousa march music rocketed through the room. Katherine was sure she saw the windows bulge out from the noise. Steve shouted in her ear, "They practice every day." Katherine nodded weakly.

The girls began to march in place, their white-sneakered feet stepping in tandem. Then as the music blared on, they leaped and swung their arms in perfect unison, pointing and gesturing to imaginary irate drivers. They frequently punctuated the routine with the shrilling whistles, the high-pitched sound nearly finishing what the loud music had begun with Katherine's eardrums.

Through it all, Steve grinned, moving in time to the music. Katherine knew it was just an expression of his enthusiasm, but each time he moved, it unsettled her. His nearness seemed to set the world atilt until even synchronized teenage traffic cops seemed like nothing out of the ordinary.

Finally the music faded in a blare of horns and tumble of drums. Her ears still ringing, Katherine managed to smile politely at the girls and congratulate them on their win. But Steve's arm had somehow ended up draped across her shoulders by the time the girls raced each other upstairs.

She sat bolt upright, jerking away from him. "We have to do something about Cora."

He leaned back into the corner of the sofa, looking almost nonchalant. "I think we've handled the situation pretty well."

Katherine locked her hands together, placing them primly in her lap. "But she can't keep breaking the rules."

He gazed at her sidelong. "Maybe you're being a little too hard-nosed."

Katherine stiffened. "Are you against rules, Mr. Walker?"

"Of course not." He waved, as if that were a trivial issue. "But some of your rules seem to be more for the benefit of adults than children."

Katherine knew that was true enough, but she wasn't about to tell him that. "The teachers need to keep order. With thirty students to a classroom —"

"Stop," he said, holding up his hand. Katherine's eyes widened. What outrageous thing would he say next? "Let's not talk about thirty kids. Let's talk about one — Cora," he said softly, roughness edging his voice.

Katherine nodded, mute, and his hand dropped away again. He told her, "That little girl went through hell in Guatemala. She saw things that no child should at her age."

"But the other children —" Katherine began, then fixed her eyes on his, as if warning him not to argue. "Some of the others have had it pretty rough right here. That doesn't mean we should let them do whatever they please."

He narrowed his eyes impatiently. "Of course not. But a rule that works for one child may not work for another."

"We can't have different rules for different children!"

"Why not?" he asked stubbornly.

"Because . . ." She blinked, waiting for the words to come to her. "Because . . ." His question seemed so simple. Why couldn't she think of an answer? To her dismay, she fell back on one of her mother's platitudes. "We must have consistent rules. Otherwise, we'd have anarchy."

"I say love should take precedence over consistency," he said, wiping away her reasoning with one preposterous, tantalizing statement.

She opened her mouth to respond when the sudden, excited cry of "Daddy!" erupted from upstairs. Steve turned and took a breath as if to call out a reply.

Then with a shudder that rattled the windowpanes, another explosion blasted through the house. On the heels of that noise came Corazon's terrified scream.

His face wild with horror, Steve vaulted over the sofa and scaled the stairs three at a time. Katherine rounded the sofa, and raced after him.

Chapter 2

Katherine was only halfway up the stairs by the time Steve had propelled himself around the top newel post and down the hall. Katherine ran after him, the gallery of family photos and ornate mirrors a blur in the long hallway.

Steve skidded to a stop at the end of the hall, and Katherine rammed into him before she could stop herself. He staggered, his arms full of her as she ended up wrapped around him.

Not bothering to disentangle her, he dragged her through the open door at the end of the hall, as Katherine realized her shoes were somewhere behind her in the hall. She gave the small bathroom a cursory look, glimpsed a gaunt, bespectacled figure — Cousin Denny? — and Corazon sitting in the bathtub, awash with red.

Oh, God, she's bleeding, Katherine thought, squeezing her eyes shut as her stomach lurched.

Still clinging to his shoulders, she marshaled her wits, since he seemed to be in shock. "I'll call 911."

Steve flicked a glance down at her. She realized with a jolt that he seemed to be holding back a smile. His eyes danced with delight.

"No need," he managed with a grin. Then a chuckle worked its way up from his chest, one that shook his body. He leaned up against the doorjamb, laughing. Confused, then angry, Katherine moved away from him to see what was so funny.

Corazon sat in the bathtub, a startled look on her face, red trickling down her cheeks and dripping from her dark hair. More red stained her white T-shirt, pooled in a pair of plastic safety goggles around her neck.

"Why are you laughing? She's bleeding!" Katherine shouted at Steve, her voice echoing in the small bathroom.

He just kept laughing, shaking his head, wiping away tears. She heard another guffaw, like a moose call, and whirled to see an odd individual that could only be the mysterious Cousin Denny folded over with mirth, his thin, salt-and-pepper hair falling across his forehead. Even Cora, red fluid still trickling down her cheeks, burst into childish giggles.

"Ms. Tipton," she said, her high-pitched

voice teasing, "this isn't blood. It's Starbaby soda."

Katherine swallowed back her queasiness with an effort. "Starbaby soda?"

Steve managed to squelch his laughter. "Strawberry soda. That's what all that red stuff is."

Katherine took a cautious step closer and touched a finger to the red liquid smearing the white-tile shower stall. "Cora's not hurt?"

Cousin Denny gently pushed aside Cora's bangs. "She got in the way of the bottle cap trajectory. Banged her on the forehead."

"Let's take a look," Steve said, brushing past Katherine. A frisson of physical awareness shuddered down Katherine's spine, adding to her confusion.

Steve sat on the bathtub edge, turning Cora's head. His thumb passed lightly across the angry pink lump just below the girl's hairline. "You *were* wearing your goggles, weren't you, *mija?*"

Cora looked offended. "Of course, Daddy."

"She sure was," Cousin Denny confirmed. "I just pushed 'em out of the way to check the damage."

Cora nodded solemnly, then craned her

neck up at Katherine. "I always wear my goggles when Cousin Denny blows up bottles."

Katherine could only stare. Safety goggles? Blowing up bottles?

She had to clear her throat twice before she could speak. "You're making explosives?"

Cousin Denny guffawed again, then reached into the bathroom sink. It was filled with ice, Katherine realized, and a half dozen glass soda bottles filled with red liquid.

"Soda," he said, pulling a bottle free. He held it out to Katherine. "I make all kinds — orange, strawberry, grape, root beer."

"I see," Katherine said, although she didn't. She took the bottle from him, holding it gingerly, as if it would detonate in her hand.

"No danger from that one," Cousin Denny reassured her. "That's a low-carb sample. Part of the control group. Here, I'll show you." And he took the bottle back and shook it vigorously.

Katherine couldn't help her whimper as she backed away. Somehow her feet tangled with Steve's, and she ended smack up against him. He threw one arm around her, the other bracing him so they didn't fall into the tub. Even as her mind told her not to, Katherine's body leaned blissfully into his hard chest, nestled against the muscular firmness of his thighs.

It was his hand curving just below her breast that woke her up. She sprang to her feet, her cheeks warming as she looked back down at Steve. He smiled, his coppery eyes bright — with humor and something else that reached inside Katherine and made her breath catch in her throat.

Then Cousin Denny released the cap on the soda bottle and a shower of strawberry soda burst from the bottle. The sound of the soda fizzing and puddling on the white-tile floor jolted Katherine's attention away from Steve.

Corazon squealed with delight. She reached out for a hand up from her father and climbed out of the bathtub. Grabbing paper cups from the dispenser by the sink, she held them out for Cousin Denny as he poured. She passed a cup of soda first to Katherine, then her father, before she took one for herself.

Katherine breathed deeply to gather her self-control. Then she made the mistake of watching Steve drink, her eyes riveted to the strong motions of his throat. She distracted herself with the soda, taking a cautious sip.

The deliciously tart taste surprised her. It was nothing like the sugary stuff that usually came in a can.

"You made this?" she asked after she'd finished the sample.

Cousin Denny nodded, pushing gold-rimmed glasses up on his nose. "Easy as pie. Trick is in the yeast. Too little and you got no fizz. Too much and watch out — carbonation rockets."

The noises Katherine had heard downstairs began to make sense. "So those bangs and pops . . ."

"My high-carb samples," Cousin Denny confirmed. "I'm looking for just the right balance of yeast and sugar. Makes the perfect soda."

Steve took the bottle from Cousin Denny. He leaned over to fill Katherine's cup, steadying her hand with his as he poured. Katherine jerked at the contact, spilling soda on her hand. She chanced a look at Steve. He gazed at her hand as if he wanted nothing more than to sip the drink from her skin.

Katherine sipped her cup of soda as Steve calmly served himself another helping. "I keep telling him that what he's got now is pretty darn good, but Cousin Denny's such a perfectionist."

"What do you plan to do when you get it right?" Katherine asked, proud at how nearly she'd controlled the trembling in her voice. "Market it?"

"Market it?" Cousin Denny looked puzzled. "Sell it, you mean? Oh I don't want to sell it."

"Then why . . ." Katherine flung a hand out, gesturing around the bathroom. "Why all this testing?"

Cousin Denny shrugged. "Research, I guess."

Cora loudly sipped the last of her soda. "Cousin Denny's always 'sperimenting."

Steve tipped the bottle toward her. "Can I give you more?" he asked.

Katherine took one look at the irresistible curve of his mouth and quickly shook her head. She turned resolutely back to Cousin Denny. "Are you a scientist then?"

"Nope." Cousin Denny swirled the inch of soda left in the bottle, eyeing the sludge his motions kicked up. "Don't like the looks of that yeast."

"Cousin Denny just likes to experiment," Steve said. "He spent the summer raising dandelions."

"Raising?" Katherine managed. "Dandelions?"

"*Taraxacum officinale,* actually." Cousin Denny gave the bottle another shake, then dumped its contents down the bathtub drain.

Steve laughed, the sound warm and rich. "Drove my father half-mad. Dad spent all of July and August pulling 'em, but Cousin Denny just kept planting more."

Katherine put a hand to her temple to try to rub some sense into her brain. "Why, er . . . why . . ." She couldn't quite figure out a tactful way to phrase the question. Obviously Cousin Denny was slightly unhinged.

"Studying seed dispersal," Cousin Denny answered. "Propagation rate."

"I . . . see . . ." Katherine murmured.

Steve grinned. "That's Cousin Denny. Just loves to experiment."

"All done?" Cora asked. When Katherine nodded mutely, the little girl plucked the paper cup from her and slam-dunked it in the tiny bathroom wastebasket.

"Ms. Tipton," Cora said quietly. "You're steppin' in the soda, Ms. Tipton."

Katherine stared stupidly at her feet as something cold and wet finally registered between her stockinged toes. Somehow she'd planted herself right in the middle of a puddle of red.

"Oh!" she said, stepping hastily back.

"Sit down on the tub," Steve said, reaching for a towel. He grinned wolfishly. "I'll help you clean them off."

"No thank you," Katherine replied primly, seizing the towel from his hands. "I can do it myself."

She stepped inside the tub and sat on the edge with her back to him. As she rinsed each foot under the faucet, she was aware of his amused grin without even looking. She dried her feet on the bathmat first, then gave them a few swipes with a towel, her hands slowing as she imagined Steve performing that service with sensual attention.

She bit back the image, giving herself a mental scolding. Knees pressed tight together, she turned and lifted her feet over the edge, taking care to keep the red lace slip under control and under her skirt. Skirting the soda pond and Steve's disconcerting presence, she left the bathroom, leaving damp footprints in her wake as she looked for her shoes and slipped them on.

It was only once she stood in the hallway, staring down at the profusion of cabbage roses on the carpet runner, that she realized nothing had been settled about Corazon. Agitated, she finger-combed back her sleek, black, chin-length hair. The prospect of yet another go-round with Steve Walker was both appalling and all too appealing.

She rounded on her heel and took one step back to the bathroom before she suddenly found her arms full of him. Her hands flexed involuntarily on the warm flannel of his shirt before she snatched them away.

She backpedaled, increasing the distance between them. "Must you sneak up on a person, Mr. Walker?"

"Steve," he reminded her. "I thought you'd gone downstairs."

Corazon nudged under his arm, safety goggles still around her neck, face sticky with soda. "Can I help Cousin Denny clean up?"

"Drink up the rest of the soda, you mean." Steve eased the goggles over her head. "Go take a shower, *mija,* and get into clean clothes."

Cora scowled, mouth open as if to protest. "Cora," Steve warned. The little girl wriggled in rebellion, but when Steve pointed down the hallway, Cora stomped away without a word. She ran the last few feet and disappeared into a room at the other end of the hall.

"Showers," he mused. "A fate worse than death to a second-grader."

"Worse than fooma bugs?" Katherine asked, surprising herself with the question.

Steve laughed. "Fooma bugs are a piece of cake to a second-grader. They have it all over us old folks when it comes to computer games."

"I really wouldn't know," Katherine said loftily. She clamped down on the little flutter inside that Steve's laughter incited. "I've never played a computer game."

His eyes widened in mock horror. "Never?"

She shook her head in response.

"What about video games?" he asked.

She shook her head again. "No video games, no computer games."

"Arcade games?"

She gave him a scathing look. He smiled down at her, and said in a musing tone, "No, I guess you wouldn't."

"I've never even been inside a video-game arcade," she told him.

"You must not have kids, then," he said, still with that contemplative smile.

"No," she confirmed. "And if I did, I wouldn't permit video games in the house."

He leaned back against the wall, arms crossed over his chest. Katherine's eyes strayed to the vee where his shirt parted. She could just make out the sandy curls that started there.

"Some computer games are educational," he commented, and Katherine's eyes snapped back up to his face. His mouth folded into a smile as if he knew exactly what she'd been contemplating.

"Computer and video games are junk food for the brain," she replied starchily.

He cocked an eyebrow at her. "They're fun. And most of them — at least mine — are challenging enough to give your mind a good workout."

She merely sniffed. Steve studied her for a moment and then he took her arm. "Katherine Tipton, you come with me," he said firmly. His grip was gentle but strong as he guided her down the hallway.

She trotted beside him. "Where are we going?"

"To my room," he replied.

Her mind raced in a thousand crazy directions she didn't want to go in. "Why?" she squeaked.

"Because it's time you lost your innocence," he snapped, and Katherine tripped and would have fallen if he hadn't had a good grip of her.

"It's a little late for that," she managed, then wished she hadn't said that when he halted and grinned at her.

But he just tugged her arm and headed off again. "Not for what I have in mind," he muttered. Katherine shivered, wondering just what that might be.

He pushed open the door at the end of the hallway and pulled her inside. Katherine sighed with delight at her first glimpse of the room. The expansive space extended nearly the width of the house. Tall windows filled the far wall from ceiling to cushioned window seat. She could see a black oak in the backyard spreading its leafless branches toward the house.

Katherine turned, taking in the room's matte-finish oak dresser and night tables, the green-striped wallpaper. Then her gaze stopped on the massive king-size four-poster. Katherine couldn't take her eyes from the bed, or from its plush, hunter green velvet spread.

Surely he didn't expect her to hop between the covers with him? As she gazed down at the immense bed, a brief, not unwelcome fantasy of herself in Steve Walker's arms got the better of her.

"I'm ready," he said, his hand cupping her elbow.

She swallowed back a gasp as her heart raced at the contact. *I'm not,* she wanted to shout, although her traitorous body certainly was. "R-ready?" she stuttered.

He tipped his head to the opposite side of the room, away from the bed. "I've got the game up on the computer."

Feeling like an idiot, Katherine saw for the first time the elaborate computer setup on an antique oak desk. Mortification flooded her at the images that had danced in her brain. Thank God the man didn't read minds.

"Let's take a look," she said briskly as she crossed the room to the computer.

She sat in one of two office chairs by the desk, smoothing her skirt with care. When he took the other chair for himself, she slanted him a sideways look. His expression was neutral as he reached for the mouse, but one corner of his devilish mouth still tipped up slightly.

Damn the man, Katherine thought as she turned her attention to his hand manipulating the mouse. Even the flexing tendons on the back of his strong hand fascinated her. With an effort, she transferred her focus to the colorful pattern on the mouse pad. Printed on a purple background was a four-inch yellow star inscribed with a hot pink heart. *HeartStar Productions* was written above and below the star.

Even Katherine recognized the HeartStar logo — the company was one of the state's top ten manufacturers of computer games as well as one of the region's biggest employers.

Steve rapidly clicked items on the screen with the mouse. "I'll start you off with an easy one."

The screen filled with an image of the yellow star and pink heart. Then the logo disappeared, replaced by *Bobo's Marble Maze* and a dizzying animation of multi-colored marbles dashing across the screen.

"Try low-speed mode," Steve said, running through the menu selections. Then he pushed aside the mouse and gestured to her. "Just click with the mouse pointer where you want the marble to go in the maze."

When she didn't move, he leaned close, challenging her, "You do know how to use a mouse, don't you?"

She scooted a little away from him on the wheeled chair. "Of course I do. I just need some room." She flicked her hand at him.

With a sardonic grin, he pushed back, giving her a foot of breathing space. She would have preferred more — a couple miles, say. But she nudged into the space he'd left her and put her hand on the mouse.

Actually, she was quite skilled with computers, well used to spreadsheets and databases, word processors and scheduling software. She'd never tell Steve, but she'd secretly yearned to try out the solitaire game when she'd first installed her computer; it took her sternest willpower to delete it from her hard drive.

She scanned the colorful screen before her, taking in the lines of the simple maze. Next to the word *Start,* a bold red arrow blinked above a purple marble. The correct direction seemed clear; it was a straight shot all the way to the right of the screen.

Confidently, she moved the mouse pointer to the right-hand corner of the maze. She clicked, and the marble moved slowly in that direction. But halfway down, where a part of the maze blinked bright blue, the marble dropped out of sight, and a grinning monkey filled the screen.

"Hey!" Katherine winced at the snide, computer-generated laughter. "That's not fair!"

"You violated the first rule of computer games," Steve said, reaching across her to return the screen to the original maze. "Read the instructions first." He handed her back the mouse. "Click on *Help*."

She did as he suggested and quickly skimmed the text. "So the blinking blue sections are traps. But how do I get past them?"

Steve pointed to the screen. "You go around them. You have to figure out detours that avoid the traps but get you to the end eventually." He cocked an eyebrow at her. "I'm afraid you'll have to *think*. Some computer games require that you do."

She scowled at him and laid her hand on the mouse again.

He merely looked down, without saying anything more, challenge clear in his face. Katherine scrutinized the maze once again. "Are the green sections a way to another dimension?"

She expected him to tease her, but he nodded approval. "That's right. Now you're using your intuition. You might be ready for the more advanced stuff."

She directed her marble past the section of solid green. "You're still talking as if this were somehow related to real life. As if this game had any importance."

"Watch out," he said, when she started to turn her marble around a corner. "There's a hidden trap there."

"Where?" she asked.

He didn't answer; his attention seemed fixed to something in her lap. With a shock, she recognized a certain hunger in his eyes.

Katherine looked down at her lap and saw that damned red lace frothing from the hem of her staid navy skirt. She vowed never to wear this slip again. It seemed to have a will of its own — a will to be seen. Her cheeks flaming, she tugged her skirt down with sharp jerks.

"What did you ask?" Steve asked, dropping his feet back to the floor.

"Where are the hazards?" she repeated pointedly.

"You're fine," he answered, rubbing a hand across the back of his neck. He tapped a few keys, concluding the game. "Clear shot."

Katherine clicked on the blinking *End* arrow that suddenly appeared and the marble rolled to the maze exit. As it disappeared, a starburst exploded on the screen and *SUCCESS* flashed in multicolored letters.

Katherine couldn't help but grin. Steve shrugged. "This game's much too easy for you."

"Oh?" she said. "Well, I'm pleased with myself. But it's not as if this were really any kind of accomplishment."

"No, but that's not really the point." He ran his fingers through his thick, sandy hair as if trying to frame what he wanted to say. "Imagine a kid with real problems, terrible problems, ones that he or she has absolutely no control over."

Katherine sighed, nodding. "There's more than one kid like that at Gardenview."

Steve swiveled his chair toward her, his knees gently knocking against hers. "A game like this — simple, uncomplicated — gives that kid a chance to have control over something. To be able to solve problems all on their own, problems that *aren't* overwhelming."

"I suppose so," Katherine said slowly. "But some of the games the kids play are terrible — violent, full of fighting."

Steve shook his head emphatically. "I don't allow games like that. I won't have anything to do with them." He tapped the monitor. "My games are all like *Bobo's Marble Maze*, or *Fooma-Fooma*, where the creatures are obvious fantasies, and imagination and intelligence are what wins. No violence."

His games, he'd said. How much time did he spend playing on the computer? She supposed he had some kind of real job, but she didn't know what it was. His personal information file at the school office said only *Self-Employed.*

Steve leaned across her to reset the screen. "Another game?"

"No thanks." Katherine pushed her chair back, and got up. "But I'm curious. What is it you do?"

He turned back to her with a grin. "Computer games."

"Perhaps you didn't understand what I meant," she said. "Computer games are recreation — not work. Exactly what do you do to make a living?"

"Computer games," he said again as he exited from the maze game and turned off the computer. "Video games sometimes, but mostly computer games."

"You play computer games for a living," Katherine said. It wasn't quite a question.

He laughed. "In a manner of speaking. Actually —"

"People really get paid for playing computer games?"

He laughed again, as if she'd told him a particularly clever joke. "Well, sometimes they do, but in my case —"

"Oh my God." Katherine stared, unbelieving, at the clock next to the computer. She held up the slim gold watch on her wrist and squinted at the minuscule face. "Good Lord," she murmured when her own watch confirmed the time. It was six-forty-five! Alan was expecting her for dinner at seven-thirty, and he hated to be kept waiting.

"I've got to go," she said, scrambling to her feet. "Thank you for, ah, an interesting afternoon." She hurried from the room and down the hall, descending the stairs as fast as she could.

When Steve reached the living room, she told him, "Call me. We'll set up another time to discuss Corazon."

"But —" he began as she headed for the door.

"Sorry, no time now." She opened the door. "Tomorrow. Give me a call."

She closed the door behind her and hurried down the porch steps. Just as she reached the end of the walk, she took another quick look at the grounds — the well-shaped photinia shrubs, the liquid-ambar trees losing the last of their golden leaves. Good Lord, the flawless emerald lawn looked as if it had been trimmed with nail scissors.

Just as that thought sprang to mind, she caught sight of someone on hands and knees at the corner of the house. The slight, older man seemed to be searching for something between the blades of grass. Then a glint of silver shimmered in Katherine's eyes, and she realized what the man was doing.

Trimming the lawn. With nail scissors.

Could he be Steve's father? The former dandelion puller?

Katherine must have made a noise because the man looked up at her and waved. He did indeed resemble Steve. Katherine entertained a fleeting image of the grass trimmer lunging after her rabidly with his nail scissors, then quickly squelched the fanciful thought.

She waved briskly at the kneeling man, as if he were performing a perfectly normal act. Then she hurried to her car, running through a list of excuses she could use to cancel her dinner date with Alan, her almost-fiancé. It had been a long and trying day.

Chapter 3

"No, Mother." Katherine cradled the phone against her ear and glanced at her desk clock. Forty-five minutes before the first of the school buses pulled up. "Alan and I haven't set a date for the wedding."

Her mother released one of her patented long-suffering sighs. "We're already half-way into October. If you're going to have a June wedding, Katherine Elizabeth, we have to start planning soon."

Rule number four of Grace Tipton's Twenty Rules of Good Conduct . . . *All weddings should take place in June.* Never mind that school activities consumed Katherine's free time from September to June.

She tried to massage away the headache gathering in her temples. "I wouldn't plan on June, Mother." She eyed the aspirin bottle and wondered if she ought to down a third pill. "Alan's too caught up with tax season in March and April, and with so many of his clients filing extensions —"

"I'd almost think the man didn't want to marry you," her mother sniffed.

More like the other way around, Katherine thought. She was the one who kept postponing the date. "It's just that we're two very busy people. Believe me, you'll be the first to know when we decide."

"I should hope so," her mother shot back. "It takes time to plan a suitable wedding."

Katherine listened with only half an ear as her mother launched into the list of tasks crucial to a suitable wedding.

"Got to go, Mother," Katherine cut her off as her eyes began to glaze over. "I want to call Alan before the kids start showing up."

She pressed the disconnect button on the phone before her mother could say another word. She wiggled her shoulders in her red, fitted jacket, but she couldn't seem to release the tension.

She wouldn't feel so rotten today if she'd slept better. But after she'd dodged last night's date with Alan with a patently false excuse and choked down a rubbery Healthy Meal from the freezer, even two hours of public television hadn't lulled her into restful sleep.

All because of *him.* Steve Walker. The quite luscious and delectable computer-game nut. When she should have been thinking of her quite respectable tax accountant almost-fiancé Alan, she instead was dreaming restlessly of a man who spent his days playing computer games.

What was the matter with her?

Katherine reached behind her to swivel her blinds shut. She slipped off her shoes, then raised her feet to her desk, adjusting her slim red skirt until she was comfortable.

As she closed her eyes, a clear image of Steve Walker came to mind, leaning over her as he directed her through Bobo's maze. Then the tension in her head finally released and she felt herself drifting off.

The buzzing of the intercom nearly jolted her from her chair. She punched the button as she blearily eyed the list of names on the phone. It was Phyllis, the school secretary on the line. "Katherine," Phyllis said with a portentousness that could only mean disaster, "Mr. Harper has called twice. He's pretty frantic."

Not even an hour into the school day and Mr. Harper was already frantic? Worse and worse. "Did he say what the problem is?"

"I couldn't quite make it out over the noise," Phyllis told her. "Something to do with Cora Walker."

Katherine's heart sank straight to her toes. "Tell him I'll be right there, Phyllis."

She stuffed her feet into her shoes — sensible flats today — and grabbed up her whistle. As she passed through the outer school office, she nodded to Phyllis. "Thanks for not putting him through."

Phyllis only rolled her eyes heavenward in response as Katherine headed out the door.

She hurried across the playground to Mr. Harper's room, the whistle bouncing in the vee where her white-silk shirt parted. What calamity had Cora engineered this time? she wondered. Had she drawn crayon murals on the walls? Decorated the ceiling with spitballs?

Of course, when it came to Mr. Harper, simply standing in her seat could have been transgression enough. Mr. Harper liked quiet, orderly children — the kind of students that were in short supply these days.

Katherine punched a tetherball as she passed the pole, dodging it as it swung around toward her on its rope. Why couldn't the elderly Mr. Harper be as flexible as some of Gardenview's other long-time teachers? Creative professionals all, they knew children couldn't always be mouse-quiet and seated in neat rows. They understood that some students learned better with hands dipped in messy finger paint, not folded in their laps.

Like Cora, a little voice reminded her, and Steve Walker's comment came back to her. Maybe he was right. There should be different rules for different children. For some things, anyway.

Katherine neared Mr. Harper's classroom. She was only ten yards away and she could already hear the noise. Children's squeals merged with Mr. Harper's vain shouting for quiet. Laced through the cacophony, a deep bass thumping roared from a boom box turned up full blast.

Katherine squared her shoulders and entered the room. Desks had been shoved aside and in the middle pranced a massive purple polka-dotted monster. Off to one side, Mr. Harper seemed on the verge of apoplexy. And dancing along with the happy children was the man Katherine had somehow expected would be at the center of it all — Steve Walker.

When Steve saw Katherine standing in the doorway, her slim figure backlit by the brilliant October sunshine, he had a clear image of a cartoon heart with wings, shooting into the heavens. Grinning like an idiot, he jolted to a halt and stared at her, imagining that little heart flying all the way into the stratosphere.

Gyrating behind him, Cora bumped into the back of his legs when he'd stopped. "Daddy!" she complained, giving him a dirty look before wriggling around him, continuing the silly dance.

"Excuse me, please," Katherine shouted barely above the noise as she stepped inside. "Hello!" she singsonged out.

The children ignored her, and an annoyed expression fleeted across her face. She gazed around the room, her eyes falling on Steve for a single, irritated second before she saw the boom box Steve had set on Mr. Harper's desk. Intent on her goal, she threaded through the delighted, dancing children, her behind a delightful eyeful in her snug red skirt.

In the same moment that she snapped the tape player off, she poured what must have been all the air in her lungs into the whistle around her neck. In the ringing silence that followed, she enunciated in a tight whisper, "Quiet. Now!"

Even Steve's spine snapped straight at the she-who-must-be-obeyed tone of her voice. The children, wide-eyed and serious, scurried to their desks. Steve's rent-a-monster didn't seem to have gotten the message though, because she continued to bob and weave to some silent music of her own. Katherine marched over and clapped a hand on the creature's shoulder.

"Don't move," she said with deadly intent. The monster froze.

Steve moved to stand next to Cora's desk and watched Katherine's radar seek him out. As she marched over to him, the chin-length black silk of her hair bobbing, Steve squelched his goofy smile of pleasure, masking it with a slightly amused expression. Then he caught her delicate, flowery scent, and breathed in deeply, just before she got to him.

She fixed her eyes on his, chin thrust forward. "What is going on here, Mr. Walker?"

"It's Cora's birthday." He swept his gaze across her face, recalling the features that had kept him up half the night. "We're just having a little party."

Katherine scanned the room, taking in the dangling balloons, the mountainous birthday cake, the swaying polka-dotted monster. "If this is little, I'd hate to see a full-scale blowout." She flicked a glance at

Mr. Harper. "I assume you cleared this with Cora's teacher."

Steve crossed his arms over his crazily beating heart as he leaned against his daughter's desk. "Of course."

"I beg to differ, Ms. Tipton," Mr. Harper piped up. He raked back his thinning hair with bony fingers. "When Mr. Walker spoke of celebrating Cora's birthday, he never mentioned the . . . the . . . extent of the festivities."

Katherine cocked a brow at Steve, then gestured to the creature. "And what is that?"

Cora turned in her seat to face Katherine. "That's a fooma bug, Ms. Tipton. From one 'a Daddy's computer games."

Katherine studied the costumed monster from its six-eyed head to its fourteen toes. "I see the resemblance now." She spun back to confront Steve. "Mr. Walker, student birthday parties are restricted to after lunch. I'm sure you understand the hazards of feeding a roomful of six- and seven-year-olds cake at nine-thirty in the morning."

He dipped his head at her. "I was aware of that particular rule, Ms. Tipton. However, I have an engagement at lunchtime." He turned to the teacher. "Mr. Harper,

Cora's promised she won't cut the cake until she has your okay."

That last statement seemed to calm even Mr. Harper's double-espresso edginess. "Well," he said. "Well, in that case . . ." Then he stiffened his spine, tugging the lapels of his worn brown double-knit jacket. "But the music is simply too loud."

"I agree," Katherine said as she brushed past Steve and moved over to Mr. Harper's desk. "And the classroom walls are thin. I'm sure Mr. Walker won't object to reducing the volume."

Without waiting for Steve's response, Katherine turned the volume knob down, then restarted the music. As the fooma bug resumed its bobbing, weaving dance, Katherine turned the knob on the tape player one notch lower. Steve followed her graceful motion as she crossed to the front of the class and took up a post by the whiteboard.

Cora nudged Steve in the ribs. "Can we dance again, Daddy?"

"It's not up to me, *mija*," he told her with only half his attention, his eyes still on Katherine. "Ask your teacher."

Mr. Harper granted somewhat reluctant permission, and the children rejoined the monster's swaying dance. Although more subdued, the party was back in full swing.

Steve wandered over to the whiteboard, leaning against it next to Katherine. They stood in silence for several minutes, watching the excited children.

The song ended and another began. “Somehow, Mr. Walker,” she said, a tiny bit of amusement mingling with the censure in her tone, “even when you follow the rules, you break them.”

Steve took heart in that shred of humor. “I just wanted to make the day special for Cora. I’m busy most of this afternoon and I have a local business function to attend this evening. This was my only opportunity.”

She looked up at him, warm concern in her vivid blue eyes. “I know single parenting is tough. But this seems like an awfully expensive way to assuage your guilt. I know these costumed characters don’t come cheap.”

He gazed down at her in bemusement. She still thought he was some kind of loser Mr. Mom who played computer games all day long. “I got a special deal on this one,” he assured her. Actually, Crystal, his nieces’ teenage friend inside the suit, had wheedled extra money out of him for this gig.

The music faded away again and the costumed Crystal waddled over to her backpack. "Who wants an animal balloon?" she shouted, her voice muffled by the suit. With excited squeals, the children gathered around the monster.

Crystal deserved the extra money she'd asked for, Steve decided as her clever hands produced a *Tyrannosaurus rex*, complete with terrifying squeak.

"Look at the kids," Katherine murmured, gazing at the rapt children with a tender expression. "He's very good."

"She, actually." Steve shifted, rolling his shoulders as if stretching were his intent. Then he settled back again, lounging as close to her as decency would allow. "I only hire the best."

Katherine glanced up at him, a hint of pink coloring her cheeks. Her floral scent hung in the air between them, a tantalizing tease. Steve could swear the room temperature had spiked upward, and he shoved up the sleeves on his pale yellow sweater.

"Oh, look!" Katherine cried, and she laid her hand on the ropy muscles of his forearm. She stared down at her hand as if she wondered how it got there before snatching it away. "A balloon butterfly," she said, her voice high, breathy. "For Cora."

Steve expected to see the imprint of her hand on his skin; he could still feel it there. As he gazed down at Katherine, at her parted lips, the darkening blue of her eyes, a vivid image burst into his mind — bare skin, whispered words, an intimate evening . . .

Steve pushed away from her. "Are you busy tonight?" he blurted out, then stood in stunned surprise at what he'd said.

"What?"

Katherine's eyes narrowed, and Steve almost wished he could take back the words he'd spoken. He hadn't felt this awkward since he was Crystal's age. "That function I mentioned —" He thrust his hands in his pockets, then pulled them out again. "I can bring a date."

Katherine's chin lifted. "Mr. Walker, it would be entirely inappropriate for me to date the father of one of my students."

"Don't consider it a date then," he said hastily. Why did he have to sound so damn desperate? He pasted on a grin. "I need a companion to liven up what would otherwise be a very dull evening. You could consider it an act of charity."

Katherine's look would have stopped a fooma bug in its tracks. "I'm afraid not," she said primly. "I'm going out with my almost —" He could see her bite back the word. "With my fiancé." Steve couldn't bear the thought of sitting through another Chamber of Commerce meeting while Katherine went off with some mysterious fiancé.

The word "almost" made Steve feel a tad more hopeful. "You're engaged," he said, sauntering back over to her. "When's the happy day?"

Katherine froze into deer-in-the-headlights stillness. *Curiouser and curiouser,* Steve thought.

She looked away. "We, ah, we haven't set the date."

Steve couldn't help but grin as he looked down at her hands, bare of jewelry. "No ring?"

Katherine whipped her hands out of sight, crossing her arms over her chest to hide them. "Not yet," she muttered.

He was unaccountably pleased with her reaction. "If you were engaged to me," he told her, "I'd damn well make sure you had an engagement ring."

"Daddy!" Cora called, pulling Steve's attention from Katherine. "It's hug time!"

Steve waved to his daughter, then leaned close to Katherine's ear. "A piece of advice, Ms. Tipton," he murmured. "Don't marry a man you don't love."

Her mouth dropped open. "You know nothing about him!" she said fiercely. "Alan's kind and loyal —"

"So's a puppy," he shot back, then pushed off from the whiteboard and headed over to his daughter with a smug grin.

"Hug time!" Steve called out as he reached the costumed character.

The children surged forward, arms out to give the fooma bug a hug. "Whoa! Careful," Steve cried as the small horde threatened to upset the costumed character.

From the corner of his eye, he saw Katherine breathe deeply twice before she marched over to the crowd of children. "Mr. Harper," she snapped, "we can use your expert assistance here."

Mr. Harper squeezed out a smile. "Line up in table groups, children. Corazon, you may be first."

Corazon gazed up at her teacher solemnly. "I'm the birthday girl, Mr. Harper. I can be last."

Steve rumpled Cora's hair, full of pride for his daughter's generosity. "Good going, kid."

He smiled at Katherine and was surprised at the yearning, the longing in her face as she looked down at Cora. This woman was a stickler for rules, but it was obvious she loved children. Maybe her almost-fiancé didn't want kids?

Then a noisy squabbling broke out behind Katherine, snapping her back to attention. "Alicia!" she scolded the source of the noise. "Stop elbowing Jenny!"

"She took cuts, Ms. Tipton," Alicia complained, tossing her red curls at Jenny.

"Wait your turn, Jenny," Katherine told the blond girl.

"Yes, Ms. Tipton." Jenny chewed on the strand of hair Cora had colored black with permanent marker. "Can I go stand with Cora?"

"Certainly, Jenny," Katherine told her, at the same time admonishing the redhead behind her, "keep your tongue in your mouth, Alicia!"

Steve chuckled as he moved up beside her. "I'm impressed. You didn't even look at her, but you knew she'd stuck her tongue out at Jenny."

"Sixth sense," Katherine said, shooting another warning glance at Alicia. "A survival skill for school principals."

"Then you'll be well prepared to be a parent," Steve commented. "That is . . ." He shot her a sidelong glance. ". . . if you and Mr. Almost Right are planning on children."

"Of course we are," Katherine told him quickly, but he saw the flash of doubt in her eyes before another conflict distracted her.

"Quit steppin' on my feet!" a pint-sized whirlwind in Mickey Mouse suspenders shouted at the towering boy behind him. Little Jimmy and Big Jimmy, Steve remembered from last year. Best friends, and once in a while, mortal enemies.

"I didn't mean to, Ms. Tipton," the taller boy said. "But he's so little."

Little Jimmy nearly grew two inches in indignation alone. "Jus' 'cause you're a — a — big fatso —"

"Hey!" Big Jimmy brandished a hammy fist. "Who you callin' a fatso!"

"Big Jimmy!" Katherine said sharply. "Back off! Give Little Jimmy some space. And Little Jimmy, apologize."

Little Jimmy shuffled his feet. "Sorry I called ya fatso."

Big Jimmy shrugged, and a moment later the two were engaging in a friendly game of pokes and jabs. "Well done," Steve said to Katherine.

"Another day, another battle," she replied with a wry grin.

He indulged in a quick touch on her shoulder. "I really appreciate your being a good sport about this birthday party."

She gave him a scathing look. "What else could I do? I don't like being the bad guy for a roomful of second-graders."

He glanced over at the line of children. Little Jimmy, dwarfed by the giant fooma bug, was just finishing his hug. "Nevertheless, I appreciate it." Steve blinked. "What is Big Jimmy doing?"

Katherine turned just as Big Jimmy was backing up several paces from the costumed monster. Crystal seemed to sense what the boy had in mind because she put up a hand to forestall him.

"Jimmy!" Katherine called out. "Jimmy, no!"

With all the energy in his oversize, fifty-pound body, Jimmy took a flying leap. He flung his arms around the fooma bug as he landed, his densely muscled frame a deadweight on the already awkward costume. In the next moment, Crystal tipped over, and the costume head tumbled off. Before any helping hands could stop her, the teenager inside the costume whacked her skull on a desk top with a sharp crack.

Steve didn't even have to check to know she'd been knocked out cold.

* * *

"I'm fine, Mr. Walker," Crystal told him around a mouthful of gum that the school nurse had produced from a secret stash. Her slender arms held the ice pack firmly to the back of her head. "Honest."

Dubious, Steve pulled the Blue Ice free of her tumble of dark curls. "You've got a knot the size of a half-grapefruit back here."

Crystal stretched her coltish legs out on the kid-sized couch in the nurse's room. "I've gotten worse sliding into third." She fanned her face. "Whew, that costume is hot."

Steve pressed the ice pack back on Crystal's head, then peeked through the window that overlooked the outer office. Katherine stood next to the six-foot-something paramedic, filling out a form on a clipboard. Steve followed the movement of her fingers as she tucked a sweep of black silk behind her ear. He imagined following that same path with his lips, tracing the shell of her ear.

Crystal cleared her throat, startling him out of his reverie. "Could I get my check now, Mr. W?"

"Check?" Steve muttered, sparing a glance at Crystal.

"For the monster gig," she reminded him. "You said you'd pay me right after."

"Sure." He groped for his checkbook, fingers passing over his back pocket twice before he found it.

"Three hundred, right?" Crystal said.

"Uh-huh," Steve agreed, only dimly aware of the sum she'd asked for. Steve flipped open the checkbook. "Three hundred."

Half his attention on Katherine as he scrawled Crystal's name, he didn't let go of the tension in his shoulders until the paramedic finally left. Then he stared down unbelieving at the check he'd just written.

"Nice try," he said wryly to Crystal as he voided the three hundred dollar check.

The girl laughed, freckled cheeks dimpling. "I wouldn't've kept it, Mr. W. Just thought I'd try."

He just grunted as he wrote a new check for the amount they'd agreed on. He tore it off and handed it to her just as Katherine reentered. She hurried past the nurse's room without so much as a glance. Stuffing his checkbook away, Steve followed her to her office.

She shot him a severe look as she slung her purse to her shoulder. "I have a meeting with the school board, Mr.

Walker. I don't have time to talk now."

She ducked past him and headed back outside. He followed, feeling like a guilty schoolkid, bobbing in her wake.

"You act as if this whole thing was my fault," he called after her as she headed for the parking lot.

She beeped off the car alarm of her silver BMW. "I never said it was," she said, opening the car door and swinging inside.

Steve caught a quick glance at her trim thighs before she shut the door again. She wasn't wearing the red slip today, he noted with a flash of genuine regret. She started the car, then rolled down the window.

Steve leaned inside the car. "I had no way of knowing what Big Jimmy would do."

"You set yourself up for catastrophe, Mr. Walker," she snapped, flipping the gear-shift into reverse. "And I'd prefer not to have any more of those catastrophes at my school." She backed away and peeled out of the parking lot.

He watched her pull away, fighting the urge to stomp his feet. Maybe he didn't need prissy, close-minded, uptight Katherine Tipton in his life, after all. Red slip or no red slip. He spun on his heel, retracing his steps to the office.

Then he remembered her long legs and nearly banged into the closed office door. He opened the door with exaggerated care, then headed for the nurse's room.

Crystal took one look at his stormy face and grinned. "Lover's quarrel, huh?"

"If you don't want me to sew you into that fooma-bug costume forever," he said menacingly, "I suggest you keep quiet."

"Yes, sir," Crystal agreed, although her lively eyes spoke volumes. She unfolded herself from the couch without another word, unsuccessfully hiding her grin. As she followed Steve out to his classic red Mustang, the look of anticipation on her face signaled him that his twin nieces would know all about Ms. Tipton by noon.

To forestall the inevitable, he delivered a pithy lecture on the evils of gossip when he dropped Crystal off at the high school. But he knew from the teenager's delighted grin that he'd only made matters worse. Then when he took his first bite of the cheeseburger he'd picked up on the way to the HeartStar Productions facility, most of the topping squished out into his lap. He traveled the six miles of country road that led to HeartStar plucking pickles and lettuce from his jeans.

Finally he pulled into his parking space

and shut off the engine, climbing out to finish his cleanup job. As he brushed off the last of the lettuce, he gazed around him at the rolling golden hills. Despite his dark mood, he felt a surge of pride at what his ten years of hard work had brought him.

He'd come a long way from the audacious twenty-four-year-old computer nerd who'd birthed a computer game business in his father's garage. Walker Enterprises, as he'd called it then, outgrew that cramped space pretty quickly, functioning in a series of rented offices, each one bigger than the last.

Then a year and a half ago, coinciding with Corazon's arrival, Walker Enterprises had been renamed HeartStar Productions and moved into its current home. These ten oak-studded acres, as well as the adjacent forty, were all his. He finally had ample room, plus space to grow.

He started up the walk toward the wood-and-glass structure that housed Operations, then hesitated, eyeing the low red brick building of Research and Development. Maybe he should visit R&D first — he was curious how that new chip design was coming along. But he knew he would only be avoiding the inevitable. He turned back toward Operations, girding himself for the dreaded weekly staff meeting.

He waved a fast hello to the receptionist. She handed him a sheaf of messages. "They're waiting, Mr. Walker."

"What's the climate?" he asked as he flipped through the stack of Post-its and While-You-Were-Outs.

"Ugly," she responded succinctly. "I'd rather face a roomful of my grandkids having an all-out cookie fight."

Steve sighed. "Thanks, Alice. Call Mr. Cohen back and set up something for tomorrow morning."

He stopped in his office, quickly tugging off his sweater and jeans. As he stood in his briefs, flipping through his collection of tailored dress shirts and slacks, he reflected on the days when HeartStar was a fledgling company.

Staff meetings had been free-for-all brainstorming sessions then. His marketing staff had consisted of a kid working on his MBA at Sacramento State. Some of his half dozen programmers and software designers had worked part-time while they finished school. The agreeable Northern California climate often lured the staff out to impromptu picnics in nearby parks, followed by pickup basketball games.

Now staff meetings were filled with interminable discussions of schedules and milestones, market share and product niches. He knew both the programmers who'd left last year had yearned for the creative freedom of a start-up again. Steve yearned for it himself.

Which was why he'd entered into negotiations for the struggling educational software company, EduSource. Its president, Marc Cohen, had never quite adjusted to computerized curriculum and wanted nothing more than to hand off EduSource to someone who could fix what ailed it. Steve relished the notion of reinventing the company, making it the kind of success he'd made HeartStar.

But until then . . . Steve sighed as he grabbed a fresh white dress shirt and gray dress slacks from his closet. He pulled on the clean clothes, then yanked a tie into a careless knot around his collar. Snatching up a navy blazer, he hurried down the hall to the conference room.

The battle lines had already been drawn, he could see. Arrayed on one side of the table were the programmers, marketing people on the other. The programmers wore T-shirts and blue jeans in a rebellious counterpoint to marketing's staid suits.

Each side faced the other off with a bulldog stubbornness.

They were arguing over packaging again. The marketing people insisted the Fooma-Fooma II packaging should be predominately blue, the programmers green and purple — after all, weren't those fooma-bug colors? They squabbled over that issue for an hour, then followed with an endless bitch session as to whether Creepy Critter was a politically correct monster.

"Time!" Steve finally shouted, making a T with his arms. He looked at his watch and groaned when he saw it was nearly five. "Just give me your status reports. We'll settle the packaging issue later."

As they filed out, looking like nothing more than sulky boys and girls, Steve realized he'd have to speak with the marketing staff and the programmers separately. He seemed to be spending far too much time lately soothing ruffled feathers and bolstering wounded egos.

After calling to check on Cora — his dependable twin nieces had walked her home as promised — he dragged out the weekly software status reports. Under that inch-thick stack lay the two-inch slab that was the monthly marketing report. He considered packing it in and taking the whole mess home, but then he remembered the Chamber of Commerce function he had to attend.

He'd have to get through this stuff now, or he'd never do it.

As Steve read through the dry-as-dust status reports, memories of Katherine sifted into his mind. Sharp regret lanced through him that he'd be spending the evening with a roomful of deadly-dull business men and women instead of with her. Damn her almost-fiancé anyway.

He called it quits at seven-fifteen, giving himself just enough time for a bathroom break and the ten-minute drive to the meeting. The restaurant parking lot was packed, and he had to park the ragtop Mustang way in the back. He tightened his tie again as he entered the restaurant, then buttoned his blazer as he headed for the banquet room.

The air was thick with fake bonhomie, handshakes, and slaps on the back. As Steve peeled the backing off his adhesive name tag, he scanned the room, seeking familiar faces.

There was Bob Henderson, the general contractor. Bill and Julie, the realtors who'd helped him buy his property. Fred, the bad-tempered local electrician. Katherine —

His brain did a cartwheel as his eyes snapped back. He broke into a giddy grin.

Katherine. She was here.

Chapter 4

There is a God, he thought.

There was Katherine, slender and cool in a tiered skirt and turquoise-silk shirt. She swayed a little as she spoke to the woman and two men with her, the flaring skirt swirling around her knees. She'd scooped her hair back with a silver comb, exposing the delicate shell of her ear.

Steve grinned in giddy joy.

Then the blond-haired man next to Katherine slipped an arm around her shoulders and pulled her close. Jealousy curled up Steve's spine, settled in his belly, wiped the joy from his heart. His fist closed, and he could swear his arm was pulling back to throw a punch.

He shoved his hands in his pockets. It wouldn't do to haul off and slug the almost-fiancé, even though Katherine looked as if she'd rather be anywhere but here. Even though, when she caught sight of him across the room, her face lit with excitement for one brief tantalizing moment.

Steve grinned in response. Katherine scowled and sent a *Keep Away* message with her eyes. Steve moved toward her, threading through the knots of chattering people, sidling past the round tables set for eight. Katherine shook her head, at first imperceptibly, then more frantically as he grew close. The movement dislodged the silver comb in her hair and flung it into space. Steve grabbed for it, missed, tipping it into a new trajectory.

He heard the clink, the splash, the outraged cry. He turned to find Fred the electrician glaring at him, gin and tonic still halfway to his mouth. And there, glittering between the lime and the ice cubes, was the silver comb.

"Sorry about that," Steve said blithely.

Katherine watched in horror as Steve took the gin and tonic from Fred's resisting fingers. The brief tug-of-war moved the comb from its resting place against the lime. It slithered to the bottom of the glass.

"Oops," Steve muttered as he began fishing for the comb with the flimsy red straw. Meanwhile, Fred Harper, the last person Katherine wanted to offend, the man she'd nearly persuaded to upgrade the school's computer-lab wiring at his cost, had turned twelve shades of purple.

Steve shot an apologetic grin at Fred's

unresponsive face. He discarded the straw and plunged his hand in, fingers first, almost spilling crushed ice onto the indignant Fred's lapels.

"Almost forgot Archimedes' Principle. An object displaces a volume equal to its weight in water. Sorry. Nerd talk," Steve rattled on.

Katherine placed a placating hand on the electrician's jacketed arm. "Let me get you another, Fred," she said. "Gin and tonic, right?"

With a scowl, Fred nodded and walked with her toward the bar. Katherine took her place in line, Fred at her elbow, and they waited for what seemed like eternity. She noticed that Alan had struck up a conversation with Steve and she wondered what that was all about until it was her turn to be served.

"Gin and tonic," Katherine told the blond-haired bartender when they finally stepped up to the front. While the woman mixed the drink, Katherine turned to look back at Steve. She couldn't help but smile at the engaging grin on his face, the mischief in his copper eyes.

She sent Fred off clutching his fresh gin and tonic, with a murmured apology, then moved back to Alan's side.

Steve handed her the silver comb, which she put back into her hair, giving him a look that warned him to say nothing more.

"That's my girl," Alan said, throwing his arm around her shoulders. "Nothing fazes her."

"Alan, don't call me 'girl,' " Katherine reminded him for the millionth time. Alan just laughed, as he always did. Katherine wondered if an icy gin and tonic down the back of his suit might refresh his memory. He ought to know by now that she hated to be called a girl.

"Steve's been telling us all about his video games while you were at the bar," Alan added. "I think I've nearly persuaded him to give my accounting firm a try for his next audit."

The question of why a man who clearly wasted most of his time playing video games would need an audit nagged at Katherine. But then Steve put a friendly hand at the back of Katherine's neck, and suddenly she couldn't even remember what an audit was.

"And to think," Steve said, rubbing gently, his fingers erasing the tension in Katherine's neck, "if it hadn't been for Katherine, I might never have known who you were, Alan."

Katherine imagined melting into a puddle at Steve's feet. And her almost-fiancé, her nearly betrothed, didn't even flinch at Steve's hand on her neck. He beamed at the prospect of a new client.

With a surge of self-control, Katherine ducked out of Steve's reach. She made a show of neatening her hair where the comb threatened to slip again. Then she caught sight of Steve watching her, his gaze tracing the line of her arms. Her hands faltered, and she almost lost her grip on the comb.

The ding-ding-ding of a spoon against a water glass carried through the room. "Let's get started, folks," Stan, the Chamber president, called out in a nasal voice.

Katherine sagged into her chair with relief. Now Steve would wander off to his own table, and she could focus instead on Alan and on staying awake during his speech. She turned a bright smile up toward Steve to say good-bye.

Then Alan pulled out the chair to Katherine's left. "Here you go, Steve. You can sit right here."

Katherine shoved the chair back in. "Oh, no," she said, "I'm sure Steve had plans to sit elsewhere."

Alan tugged the chair back out. "Nope.

He's promised to sit with us."

Katherine scooted the chair under the table again. "But it wouldn't be fair to monopolize him."

Alan grabbed the back of the chair. Katherine clutched the seat. They wrestled with it, bumping it against the table until the water glasses threatened to tip.

Steve stepped in between Katherine and the chair, breaking her grip. He sat, making himself comfortable before she could stop him.

"I'd love to join you," he said as he plucked his napkin from his plate.

"No, you wouldn't," Katherine hissed, grabbing at the napkin to take it from his hand. Big mistake. Her fingers skimmed the back of his hand, brushed his knuckles. A jolt of electricity skittered up her arm before she could pull away.

What was it about this man that affected her so? She should be mooning over her almost-fiancé instead of Steve Walker's coppery eyes. Where was Alan, anyway?

Katherine realized with a shock that Alan was sitting next to her on her right. He reached over to give her right knee a squeeze, the pressure on her nerves making her jump.

"Don't do that, Alan!" she gasped.

"Sorry, Katie." He patted her on the head, which annoyed her no end, and continued to work on his newfound client. "So tell me, Steve, what accounting method do you use?"

Katherine put her mind on pause, not listening to Steve's answer. The talk flowed around her, blending with the clank of glasses and the clink of silverware as waiters served dinner at neighboring tables.

A sudden thump brought her to startled awareness. She stared dumbly at the plate of rubbery chicken and limp broccoli before her. The standard Chamber of Commerce fare, but even less appetizing than usual tonight. The waiter had moved on, plopping a plate of food in front of Steve, then on around the table.

"Hey! Waiter!" Alan called out. He held his plate out. "I ordered the fish."

"No fish left," the waiter told him. "Only chicken."

"I can't eat chicken," Alan insisted. "I'm allergic to chicken. I demand fish."

As Alan and the waiter harangued each other, Katherine picked up her knife and fork and pondered the chicken. Her stomach turned slightly at the smell of the overspiced dish, but she gamely cut a small bite.

"Alan," she heard Steve say next to her, "take mine. We can trade."

Steve brandished his plate of fish in front of Katherine. If anything, the fish smelled worse than the chicken. With a grin and a hearty thanks, Alan offered his food to Steve.

Katherine chewed a tough bite of chicken, swallowing with an effort, as Steve forced his fork through his serving of chicken breast. "Allergies are tough. Get Cousin Denny within ten feet of a dog or cat, and his face swells up."

"Alan's allergies seem awfully convenient," Katherine mumbled. She'd meant to only think the words, then realized with a shock that she'd said them out loud. "I didn't mean that." She flicked a glance at Alan, but he was occupied in talking to the town astrologer, Doris, on his right.

Steve gave up on his chicken and started in on his rice instead. "Of course not," he said around a mouthful of rice.

She leaned closer to Steve, lowering her voice. "It's just that his allergies don't seem very consistent. He wasn't allergic to chicken last week. He complains about my perfume even when I'm not wearing any."

Steve tipped his head, as if to whisper in her ear. Instead he took in a slow breath.

"You smell luscious to me."

"Knock it off," she whispered, as the heat rose in her cheeks.

With a chuckle he sat upright again and stabbed his chicken. He lifted the entire piece up and held it aloft. "Do you suppose this chicken qualified for Medicare?"

Before Katherine could answer, another ding-ding-ding rang from the podium. Stan launched into a spiel about the upcoming Chamber golf tourney, tossed out a gentle reminder about dues, then proceeded with a recitation of Alan's many accomplishments.

"Give him a hand, folks," Stan said into the squealing microphone. "Alan Linden has some great tips on How to Age Your Receivables Before They Age You."

Alan scooped up his three-by-fives, threw back his shoulders, and headed for the podium. This was the tough part. For some reason, Alan's peaceful monotone never failed to lull Katherine into a near-sleep.

She pushed away her plate and groped for the coffeepot in the center of the table. Steve beat her to it, snagging the handle and flipping her cup upright.

He cocked his head at her. "Am I going to need a shot of caffeine to stay awake through this?"

Katherine shrugged, keeping her eyes on the brimming black liquid. "I just happen to be tired. I had a bad night's sleep."

He poured himself a cup. "Funny, so did I. I kept having the most incredible dreams."

About me? Katherine pursed her lips slightly to keep the words from springing out. Steve's devilish gaze left no doubt that she'd been a featured player in his fantasies.

"I don't place much stock in dreams," she informed him, suppressing a shiver.

"No?" Steve asked thoughtfully. "Haven't you ever had dreams, Katherine Tipton?"

"Every young girl dreams, Mr. Walker," Katherine said. "But I'm not a girl anymore. I've long since put my dreams away."

His eyes filled with a sadness, not for himself, but for her. Katherine turned away from him, riveting her eyes on her coffee. She took a sip of the bitter black liquid, then another, fighting an inexplicable urge to cry.

Alan droned on, his unvarying tone working its usual soporific magic on her. She took another big swallow of coffee, then set the cup down. She gripped the sides of her chair to fight the drowsiness, trying to focus on Alan's words. Her head dropped alarmingly once; she thrust it up again and opened her eyes wider.

Distantly, she heard the clink of Steve's spoon stirring sugar into his coffee cup. A buzzing started in her ears, blended with the rhythm of Alan's speech. Then her body eased into surrender, and she had the sense of curling up to sleep against something warm and soothing.

The clamor of applause jolted her awake. She blinked, trying to bring her mind into focus, and her lashes dragged against a firm, woolly surface. Her fingers flexed under her cheek — and gripped an arm. Cautiously, she looked sidelong at her pillow, then up — and met the amused gaze of Steve Walker, against whose arm she was comfortably snuggled.

Katherine shoved herself upright, quickly searching the room for Alan. He was just stepping away from the podium, shaking hands with Stan, grinning in triumph. As she reseated her hair comb with shaking fingers, she discovered Doris watching her from across the table. The astrologer's avid eyes flicked from Katherine to Steve and back to Katherine.

Steve leaned over and patted Katherine

on the shoulder. "She didn't sleep well last night," he obligingly informed Doris.

"Oh, really?" Doris said, a wicked grin lighting her face. "The moon was in Venus, you know. That explains it."

"Steve!" Katherine hissed, aiming her elbow at his ribs. He dodged her, laughing.

Katherine's outrage only cemented Doris's impression of hanky-panky between Katherine and Steve. Doris slid a glance at Alan as he threaded his way back to the table. The wheels turned in Doris's wild imagination, clickety-click.

"Oh, Lord," Katherine groaned, knowing how quickly such a juicy tidbit of gossip would get from Doris to her gullible clients. Katherine needed a preemptive first strike, a quick escape to forestall Doris's further speculation.

"Alan," she said as he pulled out his chair. "I'm really not feeling well. I'd like to go home."

The light of victory in his face faded to disappointment. "But Stan has two potential clients for me. Are you sure you couldn't hold out a little longer?"

Katherine made a show of rubbing at her temples, trying to ease the imaginary pain of a headache as an excuse to leave. "I don't think so." Katherine chanced a quick look at Doris; the woman's knowing smirk was infuriating. "Please, Alan?" she said plaintively.

Regret warred with sympathy in Alan's expression. "Of course, hon. I'll ask Stan to get me their business cards, then we'll go."

He turned to head back to the front table. Katherine closed her eyes as if to block out the bright lights of the room. So she was caught off guard when Steve called out, "I can give Katherine a ride home, Alan."

Katherine's eyes snapped open and she blurted, "We wouldn't want to put you out," just as Alan said heartily, "That would be great, Steve."

"It's no trouble at all," Steve reassured her, patting her hand where it lay on the table.

She stared down at the back of his hand, marveling. Whenever Alan patted her hand, she always felt patronized. Steve's action sent a shiver up her back, brought to mind crazy images of brushing her lips against his knuckles.

She tugged her hand free and laid it in her lap, tightening it into a fist to stop its trembling. This was impossible — if she reacted to Steve this way in a crowded room with her almost-betrothed present, Lord only knew what would happen in the intimate confines of a car. She had to tell Alan she'd recovered from her mythical headache. That she'd stay until he could drive her. But . . .

"I'd love a ride home," Katherine heard herself say. She stood up and scooted back her chair. She only barely stopped her feet from walking away from the table without saying good-bye to Alan.

She leaned over to deliver the obligatory peck on Alan's cheek, which he didn't return, then gathered up her purse and coat. Steve draped her coat over her shoulders, his fingers lingering on her neck when he pulled her hair free. Then he cupped a proprietary hand on her elbow to lead her from the room. Katherine threw a quick look over her shoulder, concerned about Alan's reaction. But he was deep in conversation with his table mates, oblivious to Steve's intimacy.

When they walked out into the October chill, Katherine pulled her coat more tightly around her. She shivered because of the cold, she told herself, not because of Steve's hand gently resting on the middle of her back. Her eyes roved the parking lot as they walked, then flicked to him in speculation.

"What?" he asked when he caught her glance.

"Just wondering what kind of car you'd drive."

He looked down at her as he guided her through the lot. "You say that as if my choice of car reflects on my character."

"In your case it's probably true," she told him. "I'm guessing you drive something reckless. Probably red."

"Good guess," he said with a grin as he led her to a fire-engine red '65 Mustang. "You do have remarkable intuition, Katherine Tipton." He beeped off his car alarm, then unlocked the door. "But how would you characterize your BMW?"

She took his hand, let him help her inside the car. She'd given up on avoiding his touch; she reacted to him whether she made contact or not.

Once he'd seated himself, she answered, "It's a dependable car, solid, not too showy —"

"But it's silver," he reminded her as he slipped the key into the ignition. The engine roared to life.

"So? It's a classic color," she said.

"But elusive, mysterious, flashy." He threw his arm across her seat back as he pulled out of his parking space. "I have a feeling it's the one luxury you allow yourself."

"I bought it used."

She gave him a suspicious look as he made his way to the parking-lot exit, but he didn't seem to care.

"Love the leather upholstery, too." He spared her a quick glance before returning his attention to the traffic on Gardenview Drive.

Her eyes narrowed. "Nothing unusual about leather upholstery."

He pulled out onto Gardenview, then had to stop for a red light. He turned to her. "It's sensual," he said, and he ran a fingertip down the lapel of her gray-wool coat. "And just the least bit hedonistic."

The look in his eyes warmed her as surely as his fingertips. She struggled to bring her focus back to their conversation. "I chose leather because it's more comfortable," she told him, her voice nearly a gasp, whether in outrage or arousal she couldn't tell.

"I suppose it is." He pulled away from the now green stoplight. "You'd want your car interior to be comfortable . . . and why not?"

His voice flowed over her, enfolding her with warmth. She closed her eyes to shut him out, but a vivid image sifted in — Steve in her arms on the butter-soft leather of her backseat. She could feel the sweat-slicked leather beneath her bare back, feel the weight of him pressing her down . . .

She dragged in a sharp breath to banish the fantasy. She had to get out of his car! She felt herself on the narrow edge of acting on her imaginings, of taking them into reality.

"My house is on Amethyst Court," she told him, forcing the words past her too-dry throat. "Off Yale, just past the soccer fields."

He nodded and eased into the left lane to make the turn. Five more minutes and she'd be home, then she could find something to do that would put him out of her mind. Clean the oven for instance, or chase the dust bunnies under the bed.

He'd just turned onto Yale when her stomach made its first protest. She slapped her hand over it as if to silence the sound. When it grumbled again, reminding her she'd hardly eaten a thing at dinner, Steve couldn't miss the loud, embarrassing rumble.

Steve turned onto Amethyst, curving around the end of the cul-de-sac. He stopped the car and turned to her. "If you ate as little as I did of that rubber chicken, you must be starving."

She shrugged, not wanting to lie with a denial. Then her resentful stomach made its emptiness known again, and she smiled ruefully. "I suppose I am."

"Then you need to fill it with something special. Before I take you home."

She gestured up at her house, looming above them on its knoll. "But you have taken me home."

"Ah, but you're not in the house yet," he pointed out with indisputable logic.

Her stomach prodded her longingly. "But don't you have to get back to Corazon?"

He looked at his watch. "It's after nine. She's asleep. I'm sure Cousin Denny read her every book in the house."

Another sharp hunger pang rolled through her stomach. Her mouth watered at the mere thought of food. "You're on."

"Great." He fished a cellular phone out of his jacket pocket, pulling away from her house at the same time. He hesitated briefly at the stop sign before rolling through it, all the while punching in a number on the cell phone.

He brought the phone to his ear. "Hey, Matt," he said, eyes on the road as he retraced his route to Gardenview. He angled a look at Katherine. "What's tonight's special?" he asked, humor lacing his tone. "Sounds good. Be there soon."

He hung up the phone and slipped it back into his pocket. "All set," he told Katherine as he sailed past the restaurants clustered near the community airport. He continued north toward Golden Valley Road.

He turned right instead of left as she expected, heading into the darkness where pastureland lay on either side of the road. Alarm tweaked her. "Where are we going?"

"To a friend's," he told her, his baritone a caress in her ears.

Katherine stared into the blackness, straining to see beyond the range of the headlights. "But there's nowhere to eat between here and Placerville."

He grinned, his teeth white in the dim light of the car. "You'll see."

A few minutes later, he slowed and turned onto a tiny gravel side road. The Mustang bounced and rocked in the potholes.

Her alarm slid into panic, tangled with an excitement she didn't want to name. "Where *are* we going?"

He caught the trembling in her voice.

"Hey," he said softly, "you're safe with me." He shot her a look, his eyes a brief glitter in the darkness. "At least as long as you want to be."

Katherine mulled over that less-than-comforting thought as Steve topped a short rise. As they leveled out, the headlights picked out a broad clearing where an expansive ranch-style house lay.

Steve edged around the house, continuing to an outbuilding back behind it. A looming shadow resolved itself into a man who approached the car as Steve pulled it to a stop.

"It's open," the beefy man said, gesturing toward the outbuilding where a porch light glowed.

"Thanks, Matt," Steve said as he swung out of the Mustang. "This is Katherine."

Katherine gave a timid little wave as she eased out of her side of the car. Steve had turned off the headlights and only the light from the porch illuminated the black night. A glow warmed one or two windows of the house thirty yards behind them, but that light didn't reach this far.

Katherine peered up into Matt's shadowy face, his already massive body made larger by the indistinct light. What skullduggery did the man perform out here in the middle of nowhere? Her stomach rumbled importunately. And when would Steve feed her?

Matt turned on his heel and headed for the house. Watching him go, Katherine didn't sense that Steve had moved beside her until she felt his hand on her elbow.

"Shall we?" he asked, tipping his head toward the porch light.

Despite her hunger pangs, she hung back. "What *is* this?" she asked him.

He cupped her elbow more fully, his thumb tracing a path she could feel straight through her heavy coat. "A swinging bachelor pad, of course." He leaned close to her ear, and said with heavy melodrama, "I plan to have my way with you."

She laughed, a high, nervous sound. He was joking, of course. Nevertheless, anxiety roiled with her hunger as she walked with him to the outbuilding.

He pushed open the door and in the next moment brilliant light from inside blinded her. She blinked, trying to focus on what the light revealed. Glittering stainless steel and ceramic tile met her gaze. She took in the industrial-sized stove, the commercial refrigerators.

"It's a kitchen," she said, dumbfounded.

What kind of kinky goings-on did Steve plan in a kitchen?

He urged her inside. "What better place to find something to eat?"

She took in the breath she hadn't realized she held, and an incredible aroma sifted into her nostrils. "Chocolate," she breathed.

"The finest European chocolate," Steve informed her. "Matt uses only the best for Sweet Somethings."

Katherine moved through the kitchen, pulling in lungfuls of the scented air. "Sweet Somethings?" she asked, one hand trailing along a marble slab countertop.

"Chocolate truffles," Steve said reverently. "The best truffles in Northern California. With some judicious marketing, soon to be the best in the country."

He unfolded a kitchen stepladder and gestured her into it. "Raspberry or orange?" he asked as he headed for a set of floor-to-ceiling shelves.

Katherine sank onto the top step of the ladder. "Raspberry or orange what?"

He pulled slim white boxes from the shelves, one after the other, checking each lid before replacing it. "Ah," he said finally, tugging a box free. "Truffles, of course."

She paused in the act of arranging her

wool coat on the top rail of the ladder. "But what about dinner?"

"Here it is," he said, handing her the box. He slid two stacked milk crates over next to her and sat down. "Raspberry and orange for dinner. Coffee and Grand Marnier for dessert."

She stared at him, certain he'd lost his mind. "We can't have chocolate for dinner."

He pulled out a walnut-sized truffle, and its orange-chocolate fragrance tickled her nose and teased her stomach. "Why not?" he asked, sinking his teeth into the delicacy.

There was that darn question again. "Because . . . because . . ." She tried to think, but the chocolate had softened her brain. "Because candy isn't food."

Steve's eyes closed with apparent pleasure. "Of course it's food."

What would his mouth taste like now? Katherine batted away the errant thought. "But it isn't real food."

Steve's tongue licked a morsel of chocolate from his curving lips. Katherine's heart nearly stopped. "You aren't supposed to have candy for dinner," she insisted.

He took another nibble of the sweet. "Why not?"

Why not, indeed? her stomach asked her. Surely there was a proscription against it in her mother's Twenty Rules of Good Conduct, something like *Thou shalt eat "real food" at every meal.* But her stomach was having none of that.

She turned to the open box. "Which ones are raspberry?"

He licked the last of the chocolate from his fingers, a thoroughly fascinating process. Then he pointed to the truffles on the left-hand side of the box.

"These," he told her. "The ones with the tiny dollop of red on the top."

Katherine selected one from the box, feeling like Persephone eating her first pomegranate seed. Then she took a bite and thought she would melt in a puddle of appreciation on the floor.

"God, this is heaven," she murmured around a mouthful of truffle. An edge of raspberry cut through the rich chocolate, the flavors mingling into sweet ecstasy.

"Try the orange," he suggested, holding out a truffle for her to taste.

She managed to nip a portion off with her teeth without touching Steve's fingers. The orange truffle exploded in her mouth, the sensation of it on her tongue nearly sexual.

Then she caught sight of Steve's hot gaze and realized chocolate had nothing on him for lusciousness. He leaned toward her slightly, filling her sight, his thick sandy hair begging to be touched, the broad shoulders and solid male flesh beneath his pure white dress shirt tantalizing.

The truffle could have been dust in her mouth. Her mind shrilled out danger warnings in her ears.

She snapped her gaze away from his, searching for a way to break the tension. "These are wonderful," she said brightly, waving the raspberry truffle at him.

Steve's eyes fixed on her lips. "You have some chocolate," he said roughly, "here." His finger brushed the corner of her mouth.

Katherine pulled back, bringing her hand up to shield her lips as she licked them clean. "Ah, thanks," she managed, her voice wobbly.

"You missed a bit," he said softly, his fingertip grazing her lip.

She hopped off the stepladder, out of his reach, shaking from the heat of his touch. "Tell me about Cora," she blurted, hoping to divert her mind from rampant fantasy.

His eyes narrowed, then he relaxed, leaning an elbow on the counter. "What do you want to know?"

"How you came to adopt her." Katherine nudged the ladder a bit farther from him and seated herself again. "What happened to her family."

He shrugged, but the action did not seem at all careless. "They all died when she was four . . . her mother and father, her brothers and sisters."

Katherine's heart contracted. "How?"

He closed his eyes, a long breath scraping out of his lungs. "Her father stumbled onto a cocaine poppy field. He reported it to the local police." Steve's gaze met hers again, his eyes hard, his face grim. "The drug traffickers made an example of him, and his family. Cora only survived because she'd wandered off to play."

His hand lay on the marble counter, fingers rigid. Katherine rested her hand gently on his. "How did you find out about her?"

"I have a friend who works in Guatemala City." He turned his hand to link with hers. "He'd seen her at the local orphanage."

Warmth pooled in Katherine's palm at the contact. "How much does she remember?" she asked softly.

"Almost nothing."

"That's good, then."

He shook his head, gripping her hand more tightly. "She doesn't even remember her mother's face. But I don't want her to forget her first family."

Katherine's thumb drifted in soothing circles across his palm. "Of course not."

"I have a picture of her mother holding Cora as a baby." His fingers relaxed under her stroking. "And I'd bring it out whenever she'd ask for it. But she hasn't asked for a long time."

Katherine's eyes locked with his, and she shared his grief for a woman neither of them had ever met. She was struck suddenly by the intimacy of the empty kitchen, how easy it would be to draw him into her arms to comfort him.

She sat up straight, tugging her hand free of his. "I'm dying of thirst." Looking anywhere but at him, she scanned the kitchen. "Do you suppose I could get some water?"

"Sure," Steve said evenly, slipping off the crates. He found tumblers for them and filled them with water from the sink.

Katherine jumped a little when he clunked her glass down on the counter. Steve nudged the crates closer to her, then sat. "So how long have you and the almost-fiancé been dating?"

Katherine fumbled the glass she'd been about to drink from, spilling a little on her dress. "He's not an 'almost,' " she said as she brushed away the moisture. "And his name is Alan."

He took a swallow of water. "I know. How long have you known him?" he prodded.

She had to concentrate to remember. "Two years, more or less."

He set down his water glass. "How'd you meet him?"

She hesitated, knowing what he'd make of her answer. "My mother knows his mother. They introduced us."

His eyes sparkled with humor. "Sounds like an old-fashioned arranged marriage."

She took a long drink, then dabbed at her lips with her fingers. His eyes followed the motion. "Would an arranged marriage be so terrible?" she asked, trying to shake off the trembling in her voice.

His warm fingers cupped her chin. "You *don't* love him, do you?"

"I care for Alan," Katherine insisted, jerking her head away. "Very much."

He took the water glass from her and enfolded her hand in his. "But there's no passion, is there? There's no . . ." He ran his fingertips up along the inside of her arm. Katherine nearly moaned aloud. "No fire," he murmured.

Katherine snatched her hand back, forced it into her lap. "It doesn't matter," she said, the words sounding false even to her own ears. "Alan's a good man. Steady. Solid."

"Boring."

Katherine glared at Steve fiercely. "Yes, he's predictable! If he says he'll pick me up at seven, he's right on time. If I tell him I want flowers for my birthday, that's what I get — flowers. Not candy, not perfume, not some afterthought he picked up on the way to my house —"

Katherine slapped a hand over her mouth to stop the flow of words. She turned her head aside, squeezing her eyes shut at the sudden sting of tears.

"Why are you crying?" Steve asked gently.

She shook her head sharply, then fixed her gaze back on him. "I — I don't have any reason to cry. Alan gives me what I want."

Steve's voice was quiet, his eyes steady on hers. "But you're not letting yourself want very much, Katherine."

She wanted to deny that, would have if Steve's cell phone hadn't chosen that moment to ring. He shot her a worried look as he dug the phone from his pocket.

His concern deepened as he spoke. "How high?" he asked, then sucked in his breath at the answer. "When did you give her the Tylenol?" He paused, rubbing his forehead. "Still won't go down, huh?"

He flicked a glance at Katherine. "Be right home. Thanks, Denny."

He pressed the phone's off button and turned to Katherine. "I've got to get home. Cora's got a 104° fever."

Chapter 5

Steve had to resist the impulse to lift Katherine bodily to hurry her along. She'd risen, had gathered up the two glasses to take them to the sink, but Steve's urgency to get to Cora nearly had him carrying Katherine to the car.

"When did she get sick?" Katherine asked as she gathered up her coat. "She seemed fine today."

He didn't say. "She was fine when I called at five." He raked his fingers through his hair as he ushered her out the door.

Steve opened the Mustang's passenger door and waited for what seemed like forever for her to toss her coat into the back and climb inside. He shut the door and raced around the car to his own side.

"Damn, I forgot," he said as he gunned the engine and pulled out with a screech. "I have to drive you home first."

"My house is in the opposite direction. Let's go to your place first and see how Cora is. Maybe Cousin Denny can give me a ride home."

"Cousin Denny doesn't drive anymore," Steve said, hesitating at the turn off Matt's gravel road. "He's a little odd, you know."

"I did notice. But I can wait until you can take me," Katherine persisted. "Let's go."

He shot her a grateful smile, then made the turn toward his house. They drove in silence, Steve doing his best to stay within the speed limit as he navigated the dark roads, his hands tight on the wheel. Having Katherine at his side eased his anxiety over Cora, and when she reached over at one point to touch his arm reassuringly, a rush of gratitude overwhelmed him. Gratitude, and another emotion he chose not to examine just then.

Only the porch light glowed when they pulled up in the drive. As they rushed up the walk, Cousin Denny opened the front door.

"Her fever's down to 102°," he said softly as they went inside. "She's sleeping."

"Thank God," Steve said as he climbed the dimly lit stairs. He felt Katherine close behind him. "Any other symptoms beside the fever?" he asked. "Do her ears hurt?"

"No," Cousin Denny answered. "But she said her stomach does."

They reached the door to Cora's bedroom. "It could be that flu that's been going around the school," Katherine suggested. "Half the kindergarten has been out with it at one time or another."

Steve pushed open Cora's bedroom door. The unicorn lamp by the bed filled the room with a gentle glow. Her face turned away from the light, Cora slept, her cheeks flushed, her hair pasted against her forehead with sweat. His heart aching, Steve entered the room and sat at the edge of his daughter's bed.

He stroked back Cora's sweat-stiffened hair. "Denny, would you get that old enamel pot in the service porch. Just in case she throws up."

Katherine sat on the other side of the bed. "What a pretty room," she said softly.

Steve looked up at the bed canopy, with its jungle animal print, at the vivid greens of the matching mural on the walls. He smiled at Katherine. "I'm not sure Cora would appreciate you calling her room pretty. She rejected all my suggestions of anything frilly or flowery. She likes to pretend she's a jaguar crouching in a kapok tree."

Katherine pointed to the bedside unicorn lamp. "I see one concession to fantasy, though."

Steve ran a fingertip down the worn shade. "Corazon contends the unicorn is quite fierce. I gave her the lamp when she first arrived. She staged mock battles, and the unicorn beat off her demons."

Katherine reached out to cover Cora's small hand with her own. "It isn't right," she sighed, "for a little girl to have the kind of fears she must have had." Katherine gazed down at Cora with such empathy, such caring, Steve felt emotion well up and catch in his throat.

He looked away, startled at the strength of his reaction. Then Cora shifted restlessly, bringing his attention back to her. He laid the inside of his wrist against Cora's temple and was alarmed at how hot she felt.

"I think her fever's spiking again." He turned to Cousin Denny as he returned with the pot. "When did you give her the Tylenol?"

Denny set the pot on the nightstand. "About an hour ago."

Steve sucked in a breath. "Too soon to give her another dose." As he worried over what to do next, he told Denny absently, "Why don't you go on to bed? I'll wake you if I need you."

After Denny left, Steve picked up the

thermometer that lay next to the unicorn lamp. He was glad he only had to fit the thing in Cora's ear; the old-fashioned glass kind would have been impossible.

A few moments later, the device beeped. Steve read the display, and his stomach sank. "It's 104° again." He looked up at Katherine. "Should we chance another dose of medicine?"

Katherine shook her head. "We'd better give her a cool bath." She rose and headed toward the bathroom off Cora's bedroom. "I'll run the water while you undress her."

"Katherine," Steve called, stopping her. Incredibly, he could feel himself blushing. "I know it seems a little silly, but would you undress her? She's so shy now, she won't even let my nieces in when she's taking a shower."

Katherine smiled. "Of course. Just make sure the water's not too cold. Just tepid."

In Cora's small bathroom, Steve started the water, then sat on the closed toilet seat as he waited for the tub to fill. He heard the soft murmur of Katherine's voice, then Cora's cranky responses. At one point, Katherine poked her head in and snatched a towel from its rack, then disappeared again.

When Katherine reappeared, she held

Cora in her arms, the towel covering her small body. Cora squinted against the bright light of the bathroom. "You can't look, Daddy," she said querulously.

"We'll keep the towel on, *mija*. I won't see a thing." He reached over to turn off the faucet, then asked Katherine, "Can you manage?"

Katherine nodded and sat on the edge of the tub. "She won't like this. That water will feel ice-cold to her." Then Katherine swiveled and lowered Cora into the water.

Cora squawked and tried to jump from the water immediately. "Daddy, Daddy!" she screamed, struggling against Katherine's hands on her shoulders.

"Get her feet," Katherine cried as the girl began to kick. Drops of water showered Katherine's face, and she shook them off. Her hair comb flew into the water.

Steve grabbed Cora's bicycling feet, holding them down. "Easy, *mija*, easy. We have to do this, you're burning up with fever."

But Cora was having none of that. She kept fighting until Steve feared his grip on her ankles would hurt her. "Cora! Lie still!" he yelled, feeling helpless to get through to his daughter.

It was Katherine who finally managed to

calm her, leaning close and murmuring soothing nonsense. Cora surrendered at last, although her body shook with sobs. One hand supporting Cora's head, Katherine pulled the wet towel back over her.

Steve released his grip on Cora's ankles, then rubbed the red marks from them. "How did you know to do this?"

Katherine dribbled water through Cora's hair, smoothing it back. "My younger sister ran high fevers when she was little. My mother and I would have to bathe her." She filled her cupped hand with water and let it run off Cora's cheeks. "Hasn't she ever had a fever before?"

Steve sank back onto the toilet seat. "Not like this. In fact, she's hardly ever sick." Cora had quieted, her eyes squeezed tight against the light. Steve flipped on the night-light by the sink and turned off the overhead. "How long do we do this?"

Katherine shifted on the edge of the tub, repositioning her hand under Cora's head. "Until her fever lets up."

"You must be uncomfortable sitting like that."

Katherine smiled, shoving her hair back behind her ear. "It is a bit awkward."

Steve rose and reached for the small step stool Cora used to reach the sink. "Here."

He scooted it close to the tub. "Sit on this."

Katherine lowered herself gratefully to the step stool. Steve grabbed the other towel from the rack and folded it. "Let's put this under her head."

Katherine tucked the towel into place, then sighed with relief, swiveling her shoulders. "When I had to bathe my sister, I used to sit in the tub with her."

Steve reached behind Katherine to retrieve the hair comb. As he fished in the water, his hip pressed against Katherine's back, and the heat jolted through him. Experimentally, he leaned closer, and waited for her reaction. At first he saw no response, then he noticed her hands, that had been busy laving Cora's temples with water, stilled. He waited for her to pull away from him. She didn't.

She's just too tired to move, he told himself. He shouldn't read too much into her inaction. Then she leaned back, infinitesimally increasing the contact. Only a moment, then she straightened away from him and resumed bathing Cora.

As his fingers finally closed around the comb, he couldn't help but grin. Katherine might never admit it, but she'd enjoyed the contact as much as he had, he'd swear it.

He dried the comb on the one remaining dry towel and held it out to her. “This comb’s spent more time out of your hair than in it.”

“Thank you.” She plucked it from his hand as if she didn’t dare touch him. “I don’t think I’ll tempt fate anymore tonight.” She slipped the comb into her skirt pocket.

A few strands of her silky hair slipped over her forehead and Steve ached to brush them back. “You’re already tempting me,” he said softly.

Her eyes widened, not with fear, but awareness. Their blue darkened, and their heat seemed to burn into him. Then she turned away. “No,” she murmured. “I’m not.”

He lowered himself to the edge of the tub facing her. He flicked a quick glance at Cora; she lay peacefully, eyes closed, body relaxed. He returned his gaze to Katherine and saw the hidden fire in her eyes.

Katherine’s lips parted as she watched him, her breathing quickened. Her hands lay restlessly in her lap, worrying the folds of her skirt. He imagined those hands on him, stroking up his arms, releasing the buttons of his shirt one by one.

“Daddy.” Cora’s querulous cry dragged

him from his erotic wishful thinking. "I don't feel good, Daddy."

He returned his wandering attention back to his daughter. "I know you don't feel good, *mija*."

"No, Daddy," Cora managed, trying to rise. "I *really* don't feel good."

Katherine laid her wrist on Cora's forehead. "She feels cooler. Can you get that temperature gadget?"

Steve rose and hurried into the bedroom. Just as he grabbed the thermometer, Cora called out imperiously, "Daddy! I want out *now!*"

He returned to the bathroom to see Cora standing, one hand clutching the towel to her, the other on Katherine's shoulder. One look at his daughter's green face told him he should have retrieved the pot instead of the thermometer.

Steve had only half turned toward the bedroom again when Cora lost control. Leaning over Katherine's lap, her mortification clear, Cora threw up all over Katherine's skirt. Her narrow shoulders heaving with the effort, she followed her moment of disgrace by bursting into tears.

Of all the responses Steve might have expected from Katherine — that she'd holler in outrage, or spring to her feet in disgust, or at the very least immediately try to clean the mess from herself — he didn't expect what she actually did. Not even looking down at her soiled skirt, she threw her arms around his sobbing daughter, whispering, "It's okay, *mija,* it's okay."

"I-I-I'm s-s-sorry, Ms. Tipton," Cora stuttered through her tears.

"It wasn't your fault, sweetie," Katherine soothed.

"But I m-m-made a mess on you."

"I know, sweetie, it's pretty icky stuff." She tightened her arms around Cora. "Let's get you out of the tub."

Steve stepped forward, reaching for his daughter. "I'll take her. You clean yourself up."

"No, Daddy, no!" Cora protested, her wet body wriggling as he lifted her. "You can't see me get dressed."

Juggling his daughter in his arms, Steve snatched the dry towel from the rack. "I won't look, *mija,* I promise." He set Cora down to drip on the bedroom carpet, then turned back to Katherine. "I'll see if I can find you something of the twins' to change into."

"Thanks," she gasped, holding her breath against the unpleasant odor in the enclosed space of the bathroom. Still seated, she reached over to swing the door shut.

After pulling out a clean gown for Cora, Steve headed for the twins' room. He grinned as he climbed the stairs to Melinda and Theresa's attic enclave. Katherine hadn't spoken a word of censure to Cora, hadn't even flinched at the stink until out of her sight. She'd handled the awkwardness expertly, lovingly, as Cora's own mother might have —

Steve stilled, one hand on the twins' bedroom door. Katherine had used the endearment *mija,* the shortened form of *mi hija,* my daughter. She must have heard Steve use it. She couldn't have known what it meant.

The thought of Cora as Katherine's daughter started a warm glow in his chest that quickly spread, filling him with an unexpected elation. Katherine as Cora's mother meant Katherine living under his roof, Katherine as part of his family, Katherine as his wife —

Whoa. Steve brought a shaky hand up to his forehead, tried to rub away his lightheadedness. *Let's take this a few steps back,* he told himself. *Wife means married. Married means . . . you love her.*

He shook his head, feeling nuttier than Bobo the Monkey. He couldn't possibly love Katherine. He'd only met her two, count 'em, two days ago. She had a gorgeous face, incredible legs, a dynamite body that kicked his libido into high gear. But that was only attraction, only sex. Men didn't fall in love with women they'd only known two days.

His father had married his mother one week after they'd met.

Steve batted that consideration aside, unwilling to give it even a moment's thought. Turning the knob with exaggerated care, he opened the twins' bedroom door. He felt his way across the dark room to Melinda's bed, bonking his head on the low ceiling halfway there. Biting back a curse, he laid a gentle hand on Melinda's shoulder to wake her.

He whispered his request twice before Melinda registered it. "Sure, whatever," she mumbled, then promptly went back to sleep.

Shuffling toward the closet, Steve ducked inside and snapped on the light. Squinting against the brightness, he scanned the disaster area that was Melinda and Theresa's closet.

Steve managed to pry a demure gray-knit top from Theresa's side to go with the one decent pair of jeans Melinda owned, then made his way back down to Cora's room. He stood at the foot of his daughter's bed a moment, watching her sleep, reassured by her even breathing.

Then he turned to tap lightly on the bathroom door. "Katherine?" he whispered.

The door opened slightly. "Here," she said, her hand groping through the opening. He handed her the clothes, and she dragged them inside.

"Good God!" he heard her exclaim a moment later.

Steve leaned close to the door. "What's the matter?"

She was silent a moment. "These might be . . . a little snug."

Steve grinned in anticipation. He leaned against the doorjamb, listening to the sounds of her dressing through the narrow opening. He heard the swish as she drew the jeans on over her legs, then the sound of the zipper. He'd never realized how erotic a zipper could sound.

Finally, she exited the bathroom, gingerly holding the bundle of her soiled clothing. "I rinsed them out as best I could."

If he'd thought blue jeans would be less tantalizing on Katherine than a micro-length skirt, he was sorely mistaken. The tight jeans hugged every curve with breathless appreciation, cupping her bottom, cleaving slightly at the juncture of her thighs.

She cleared her throat, and Steve dragged his eyes up, across the gray knit of her top. Her breasts curved under the knit with womanly grace. He let his mind drift and fill with erotic images — his hand cupping her breast, palm brushing the tight bud of her nipple under the soft knit. Then Katherine smiling up at him, lifting the top, reaching out . . .

. . . and taking a baby from his arms to bring it to her breast.

Their baby.

Steve nearly fell over his feet as he stumbled back. In Katherine's face, a mixture of annoyance and speculation played. Pointedly holding out her soiled clothes, she asked, "Do you have a bag to put these in?"

Keeping his distance, he reached out to pluck the pile from her hands. "I'll take care of them," he told her, then escaped into the hall.

He leaned against the wall a moment. A baby! Where in the world had that idea come from? He had always felt Cora filled his life. He didn't reject the idea of other children, but that thought had always gone in tandem with the amorphous *someday* when he finally met that special someone.

Someday couldn't be *now.*

Yet each time he was near her, Katherine worked more deeply inside him. His easy-to-handle fascination for her had transformed into a nearly terrifying absolute need.

It can't last, he told himself. The newness lent the attraction such power, the novelty of prim-and-proper on the surface and molten fire inside. Such a short-term passion couldn't possibly last.

Okay, okay, after a week's engagement his parents had begun the first of thirty years of marital bliss. And they would have made thirty-five this year if his mother had lived. But this was different. Katherine was just an incredibly gorgeous woman, tremendously loving under her tough veneer — and oh, Lord, that was just what his father had said about his mother.

He was a goner.

Moving with slow, deliberate steps, Steve walked down the hall to the laundry chute and dropped the skirt and blouse inside. When he returned to the bedroom, he hesitated at the door. The picture of Katherine on the edge of Cora's bed, her hand on his sleeping daughter's forehead, tightened something in his chest.

Katherine picked up the thermometer from the nightstand and held it to Cora's ear. "Nearly normal," she sighed, turning to look up at him. "With any luck it won't go up again. Guess what? She made me promise we'd take her out to Pizza Pals when she's all better."

Gazing at her, at the curve of her cheek, the warmth in her blue eyes, Steve felt a little feverish himself.

"Okay. A promise is a promise. Although how she can think of pizza after being that sick to her stomach . . ." He smiled and Katherine smiled back, dazzling him.

He drew out his hand to rub his eyes.

Was he falling in love?

Katherine's smile faded at the intensity of Steve's expression. His heat she'd become accustomed to, his passion. This was something new, a different kind of hunger as if he wanted to draw her inside him and hold her there forever.

The look frightened her. Filled her with longing. Made her wish she could hold him inside *her.*

He pushed away from the doorjamb and

moved inside, and, despite herself, Katherine shrank back a little. But he stopped at the foot of the bed and leaned against the bedpost. He glanced at Cora's bedside clock. "It's nearly midnight. Why don't I take you home?"

She didn't want to leave, wanted an excuse to stay. She looked down at Corazon, considering. "Let's wait a while longer, to see if her fever returns."

As if to put distance between them, Steve circled the bed and sat on the other side. Katherine scooted back to prop herself against the bedpost, legs stretched out in front of her. Steve slipped off his shoes and followed her lead, although that left only a few feet between them on Cora's double bed.

Katherine scrunched her bare feet into the bed's thick comforter as tiredness surrounded her like a cloak. "If you don't mind me asking," she said quietly, "how many people live here in the house with you?"

"I don't mind." Steve folded his arms across his chest. "Usually there's six, sometimes seven. Me, Cora, the twins, my dad, and Cousin Denny. My older sister Renee stays in the granny flat over the garage when she's in town."

Her exhaustion making her restless, Katherine drew her knees up and wrapped her arms around them. "The twins are Renee's daughters, then."

"Right. Renee and her husband travel, and the twins got tired of tagging along."

Laying her head on her knees, she turned her face toward him. "What kind of business are they in?"

He grinned. "They're with the circus."

She blinked, wondering if she'd heard right. "What do they do with the circus?"

He gave her a sidelong glance. "They're clowns."

Her surprise dissolved into amusement, and laughter wiped any measure of censure from her tone. "Somehow, that fits. Are there any normal people in your family?"

He shook his head.

"We've all tried to be normal at one time or another, but it didn't work out. Too much trouble."

Katherine laughed softly, and shifted to recline on the bed, her head near Cora's feet, her toes curled against the bedpost. "Tell me more," she said, encouraging him.

Steve swiveled to face her. "Are you sure you want to hear? We're not the least bit proper."

She smiled sleepily. "Tell me," she said.

Steve extended his legs and snugged his feet under her legs. "Who first?"

Katherine considered protesting, but the contact just felt so cozy, and the words wouldn't form. "Your dad."

He nodded. "Dad worked as a corporate attorney for nearly thirty years. He didn't like it much, but he was good at it."

She yawned hugely, covering her mouth with her hand. "Sorry. Go on."

He stared at her intently a moment, then continued. "When my mother got sick, Dad realized he hadn't spent nearly as much time with her as he'd wanted. He quit his job to stay home with her."

Katherine repositioned her legs more tightly against his feet. "Where's your mom now?"

"She died," Steve told her. "Six months after my father quit his job."

Katherine lifted onto her elbow and propped her head on her hand. "I'm so sorry."

Steve shrugged. "It's been five years. Anyway, he never went back to his old job."

Katherine tried to swallow back another yawn and only half succeeded. "I suppose he didn't have the heart to return."

"Yes and no," Steve told her. "It was more that he refused to continue doing something he never really liked. He decided he'd do exactly as he pleased instead."

"Which is?" Katherine prompted.

"Gardening. He gardens."

A memory nudged itself to the surface in Katherine's tired brain. "Oh!" she said, eyes widening. "I saw him. You look like him. He was clipping the lawn with nail scissors." Somehow, that didn't seem so odd right now.

A lazy smile spread on Steve's face. "Dad always was a bit of a perfectionist."

Katherine reached up to Cora's forehead and laid her wrist against it. "Still nice and cool." She curled up again on the bed. "So your dad's retired?"

"No," Steve answered, drawing out the word. "He pretty much gardens full-time."

Katherine narrowed her eyes, trying to disperse the confusion from her tired brain. "He has a landscaping business?"

Steve shook his head. "Oh, no, Dad doesn't landscape, he gardens. And not for anyone else, only for me." He tapped his chin, staring thoughtfully into space. "Actually, he did put in some rosebushes for the Clement sisters. They're in their nineties and couldn't manage it themselves."

This would make sense if I wasn't so sleepy. "Then gardening's just a hobby."

"*Just* a hobby . . . You mean like bridge, or stamp collecting or ships in a bottle?" Steve tapped his chin again. "No, I'd have to say that gardening's more of an all-consuming avocation for Dad."

Katherine passed a hand over her face. *Meltdown! Meltdown!* her brain screamed. *This does not compute!* Certain she was leading herself further down the path of lunacy, she asked, "What about Cousin Denny?"

"Oh, he doesn't garden," Steve assured her.

She fixed him with an exasperated glare. "I mean what does he do? Besides 'experiment'?"

Steve turned thoughtful again. "He reads mystery novels, and the occasional romance. He likes to butterfly watch."

"Butterfly watch . . ."

"Like bird watching, except with butterflies," Steve informed her. "But that's just a hobby."

Katherine closed her eyes and counted silently to ten. "How long has he lived with you?"

"Since he quit the State Legislature. Two, three years ago."

Cousin Denny's face floated into her consciousness and Katherine's eyes flew open. "Was he Assemblyman Dennis Walker?"

"The very same."

Katherine pushed herself upright and sat back on her heels. "Wasn't there a big brouhaha when he left? Some scandal?"

"I suppose you could say that. Cousin Denny called it scandalous."

Katherine racked her brain, trying to recall the details. "I remember! He refused his salary for the year."

Steve chuckled. "And tried to induce the rest of the Legislature to do the same."

"Because he said the Assembly wasn't doing its job."

"Cousin Denny felt the elected representatives were more concerned about their own special interests than the will of the people."

Katherine remembered the headlines. "He made quite an impression on our students. It was my first year as principal, and I made sure each teacher discussed the issue in his or her classes."

Ethics and honor, Katherine had told her students. That's what this man represents.

"Wow," she said in soft wonder, gazing up at Steve.

"Wow is right," he murmured, following the line of her slender legs where they rested near his.

They were so close. Too close. "Steve," she breathed, as a warning, as an invitation.

He shifted on the bed, turning to face her. They sat knee to knee, and the space between their bodies shivered with electricity. He gazed at her for a long moment, then he lifted one hand and traced the line of her lower lip with his finger in slow strokes.

Slowly, he moved his hand to her cheek and skimmed his palm against it. He let his fingertips brush across her ear, into the silk of her hair, and she couldn't hold back a slight gasp.

She brought her hand up to press against his chest. She intended to push him away; she didn't.

His eyes locked with hers, he leaned in closer.

Confused, Katherine took one look at his face and sudden panic lanced through her.

It wasn't the passion; she'd expected that. His eyes still seared her with their fire. It was what lay behind that heat that frightened her, the strong emotion that she read.

Katherine's brain tried to figure out the meaning of the softness that edged his touch. Her heart seemed to know the answer, spelled it out with each steady beat. But she brushed aside the message of her heart, refused to hear the solution.

Katherine closed her eyes. "I'd better go home now," she said quietly. This wasn't the time or the place for anything to happen . . . no matter how good being close to him might feel.

"Yes," Steve agreed. "Let me tell Denny we're going, then I'll take you."

Katherine waited until he'd risen from the bed before she opened her eyes. She scooted up to test Cora's temperature, holding the thermometer to her ear one last time. Normal, she noted with relief. A good night's sleep and she'd be fine.

When Steve returned, Katherine took great care not to look at him directly. She retrieved her shoes, then sidled past him out of the bedroom, preceding him down the stairs and out the front door.

"I'll get your clothes back to you next week," he said as he held the car door open for her.

She murmured something noncommittal, then swung inside the car. It took an effort not to turn to him once he sat beside her, but she kept her eyes forward on the short drive home. Once there, she slid hastily from the car. "Thank you," she said, fumbling for her purse and her keys.

"I'll wait until you're in safely."

"Thanks," she repeated inanely, and hurried up her walk. She turned her key with trembling hands and stepped into the house. Turning on the front porch light to signal that she was inside, she peeked out the window to watch him.

He seemed to hesitate a moment before he backed out of her driveway. She thought he looked at her, although it was too dark to see his face. She waited until his Mustang had turned off her cul-de-sac before she climbed the stairs to her bedroom.

She undressed methodically, peeling off the too-tight jeans with relief. She went through the motions of getting ready for bed, keeping her mind set on each mundane action as if it were crucially important.

Finally she lay in bed, fluffy white comforter snugged to her chin, eyelet lace pillow under her cheek. Like a litany, she ran the denials through her brain.

It wasn't love she saw in Steve's face. It wasn't love. It couldn't have been. He couldn't possibly love her.

Katherine flopped to her other side, resettling the comforter. He didn't love her, but if he did, it was just too bad. She was marrying someone else. A man who was steady and reliable. Who could be counted on, who was dependable. Who would never let her down.

He couldn't love her. Damn him, he didn't.

He couldn't.

I love her.

Steve stared up at the smooth white plaster of the ceiling and rolled that incredible thought around in his mind.

He remembered hearing his father tell the tale of how he met Steve's mother, how he knew, *knew,* within minutes, that here was the one, here was the love of his life. It took his father two days for his brain to accept what his heart knew, and five more days to convince his stubborn mother that she returned that love.

Steve swiped a hand over his face. He had a feeling Katherine's surrender would take longer than five days.

Chapter 6

Katherine's mother had come over unexpectedly to supervise renovations again and nag, on the very day that Corazon Walker declared herself cured of her stomach flu and ready for pizza.

A stickler for politeness, Grace Tipton couldn't very well say no when Steve and Cora asked her to come along.

When they arrived at Pizza Pals, Katherine had to squelch a laugh at the look of horror on her mother's face. Grace teetered in the doorway, mouth dropped open, saucer eyes surveying the hysteria.

Grace said faintly, "It's very . . . busy, isn't it?"

The room seethed with children, shrieking, racing, scrambling up and down the rope ladders of the jungle gym. They ran pell-mell or toddled stiff-legged from attraction to attraction, leaping into the ball room, bouncing on the moon walk, sliding on slides, swaying on suspended bridges. Their screams and laughter competed with the bing-bing-bing of electronic games and the crash of skeeball. Pizza spiced the air, competing with the scent of deep-fried foods.

Amidst the clamor, Grace stood motionless, thunderstruck. Katherine knew she ought to rescue her mother, but before she could say a word, Cora's small hand closed on one of Grace's fingers. "C'mon, take me to the ball room. Please," she appended hastily, before towing the startled Grace away like a barge.

Katherine slanted Steve a challenging glance. "Shall we?"

He leaned toward her, his mouth achingly close to her ear. "Are you hungry?"

He seemed to be about to kiss her, and there was no sick child to stop him this time . . .

She tipped her head away from him, but somehow her neck curved closer to him. His warm breath kissed her throat, starting a curl of heat low in her body.

His lips brushed her ear as he murmured, "I said, are you hungry?"

Starving, Katherine thought helplessly. *Ravenous.* But aloud she said, "Not yet. I'd rather watch the fun." She pulled herself away from him and headed toward the ball room. She wasn't ready for this, she knew that much.

Katherine serpentined through the mass of children to find her mother perched on one of the padded sides of the ball room.

Just as she reached the play area, Cora erupted from the pit of brightly colored balls, right at Grace's feet. The older woman teetered and somehow ended up in the pit next to Cora, laughing, to Katherine's infinite amazement.

Before Katherine could even figure out how to enter the ball room and help her mother out, Steve came up behind her and lifted her off her feet, swinging her up into his arms. He hopped from side to side as he struggled out of his shoes, nearly letting her go. Katherine clutched at his neck and dissolved into a fit of giggles.

When he started fumbling for her sneakers, she slapped his hand away. "Allow me," she said as she scooted them off her feet. "I'd rather you didn't drop me on my head."

By the time they clambered up the steps to the ball room together, Grace was sprawled in the pit, up to her nose in plastic balls. Steve jumped feetfirst, holding on to Katherine for dear life. Eyes shut, face scrunched into his chest, she held her breath until they came to a stop.

When she opened her eyes, she rested

just on top of the sea of balls, still in Steve's arms. Cora popped up next to them.

"Can we have pizza now, Daddy?" Cora said eagerly.

Laughing, Steve lifted Cora in his arms and rose. He cuddled his daughter close to his chest, planting a raspberry kiss behind her ear that set her to squealing. Cora's giggles and her brilliant grin tugged at something inside Katherine. Watching them, she suddenly, intensely, wished Cora were hers, wanted Steve — a man *like* Steve — at her side.

The fierce emotion still burned in her eyes when Steve looked up at her. Their gazes locked, and, for a moment, an exultant joy lit Steve's face. Entranced by it, Katherine let his joy wash over her, let herself believe the possibilities.

She caught the sudden look of disapproval on her mother's face and struggled away from him, already hearing the lecture to come. *You hardly know this man. What about Alan? What can you be thinking of, Katherine Elizabeth?*

Clutching the netting at the exit to the ball room, Katherine turned to look at him over her shoulder. He stared at her, puzzled by the abrupt change in her mood.

Katherine's lips tightened and she nodded toward her mother, glaring at him.

Please understand, she tried to tell him with her eyes. *My mother just wouldn't approve.* His expression shuttered, and he tipped his head back down at his daughter. "Hungry, huh?" He started moving toward the exit, legs sloshing through the balls. "Suppose a giant pizza would fill those empty spaces?"

Cora wriggled with excitement in his arms. "With french fries, Daddy? And a super soda?"

He reached the exit, stepping up on the padded side of the pit. His eyes sought Katherine's again, and he gazed at her a long moment. Guilt swamped Katherine as she realized that she'd hurt him, simply to avoid her mother's disapproval.

Then he turned his attention back to his daughter. "Anything you want, *mija*." He flicked a final glance over his shoulder at Katherine as he descended the steps. "Anything you want."

Katherine tried to blame the uneasy mix of pizza, fries, and soda for her queasiness on the drive home, but she knew she lied. She'd only nibbled on her pizza, picked through her fries, and wet her mouth with the soda. The source of her discomfort was the memory of Steve sitting across the table from her, as he tended to his daughter, and even elicited a ladylike chortle or two from Grace, who'd actually seemed to like him.

Her mother had even shut up on the subject of Alan, whom Katherine had expected to hear about all the way home. Was it possible that Steve had miraculously charmed the socks off her judgmental mother?

"Damn," Katherine muttered as she manhandled the car into a lower gear. She goosed the BMW up the foothill grade, giving it too much gas. The car responded with an offended roar.

"You're going to ruin your engine," Grace admonished her absently.

I don't give a damn, she thought savagely. *And I don't give a damn about Steve Walker.* She wondered where that thought had come from, and answered her own question silently. The man had turned her life upside down in a few short days, and she couldn't think of anything but him. Day and night. The nights were worst of all. She couldn't stop remembering their closeness . . . the tenderness and concern he showed for his daughter . . . the way he'd made her feel. Alan had never once, in the two years she'd known him, made her feel like that. Like she was melting all over.

Katherine simply wanted to surrender. What the heck. Fall in love. Ditch Alan. For once in her life, she wanted to kick up her heels and do what she wanted.

Even if it wasn't the right thing.

She knew, deep down in her soul, she would never do it. She was her mother's daughter, after all. Falling in love was a risky business that shouldn't be left to amateurs, Grace had often told her.

Alan was a sure thing, she knew that. Steve was a wild man at heart, unpredictable, all too available, and . . . and . . .

Dangerously sexy. Her wayward mind filled in the blank.

"Did you plan to drive right over that car?" her mother questioned mildly, jarring Katherine from her unnerving thoughts.

Taillights on the car ahead glowed three feet from her front bumper. She released the accelerator and pulled the BMW into the slow lane.

Eyes on the road, Katherine, she told herself crossly. *Banish that man from your mind.*

She'd just about managed to when the

familiar horn beeped and Steve's red Mustang roared up beside them, Corazon waving wildly and pointing to the drycleaned clothes which hung against the back window.

Oh, great, she thought wildly. *He forgot to give me back my clothes at the restaurant parking lot when my mother was busy mopping ketchup off Cora in the bathroom.*

Now she would get to play Twenty Questions with the unforgiving Grace about exactly how and why Steve was returning her clothes when she was lucky enough to have a reliable man like Alan in her life. Blah blah and so forth.

Katherine bit back her fury and waved cheerily at Corazon. The little girl beamed, and so did Steve.

"What is that man doing under your house?" Grace asked as Katherine pulled into the driveway.

Katherine looked at a pair of workboots protruding Wicked-Witch-of-the-East-style from the crawlspace under the house. "I don't know," Katherine answered slowly, not liking the portents. The workboots belonged to the contractor they had left in charge, and he seemed to be very much alive, judging by the curses he was shouting.

She eased out of the car, as if by moving carefully, the disaster she suspected could be averted. Grace had no such compunctions, however, and she moved briskly up the walk to the porch.

"There's a lake in here," she called from the open doorway. "Your entryway is flooded."

Katherine climbed up the front porch as if it were a gallows. She stared down at the dirty, soggy towels along the doorjamb and the inch of water behind them. With a low moan, she squeezed her eyes shut in despair. In a single, prayerful moment, she wished for someone to come and make it all better. Someone reliable. Someone strong. Someone like . . . A certain hot red Mustang turned onto her cul-de-sac, interrupting her.

As she watched his car curve around and park in front of her house, she couldn't quite push away the little thrill that he was here. Somehow, Steve's appearance seemed to qualify as fulfillment of her wish.

He's not for you, Katherine reminded herself as he climbed out of his car. *Alan is the one you want.*

Yet as he bent to take the drycleaned clothes from the Mustang's backseat, the motions of his lean body transfixed her. He told Cora to stay in the car, and turned to face Katherine. She had to admit she was happy to see him. When he reached the bottom of the porch steps, her face seemed to take on a life of its own, lighting in a welcoming smile.

His neutral expression took some of the wattage out of her smile. "I brought your clothes," he said, holding up her skirt and blouse in their transparent plastic bag.

"Thank you," she said lightly, taking them from him. "You could have just thrown them in the washer, you know."

He continued up the steps, not quite looking at her. He smiled warmly at her mother. "Hello again, Mrs. Tipton."

To Katherine's amazement, her mother didn't even ask about the clothes. The older woman seemed to be a lot more interested in the flood.

"You seem to have a problem," Steve said blandly, nudging at the towels with his sneakered toe. Gentle waves of water lapped away across the entryway.

Katherine hooked the coat hanger onto the porch railing, then squeezed between Steve and her mother. "I think our contractor is experimenting with an indoor pool."

Grace seemed to bristle at the mere mention of her nemesis. "That incompetent baboon —"

"Mother!" Katherine scolded, then she called out to the man, "Bob?" When his feet didn't move, she shouted, "Bob!"

Bob struggled out from under the house, brushing cobwebs as he got to his feet. His expression turned mulish when he saw Grace standing behind Katherine.

"Bob?" Katherine prompted.

Bob turned away from Grace, patently ignoring her. "I'm real sorry, Ms. Tipton."

Steve moved beside Katherine, brushing her elbow. "What happened, Bob?"

Bob tugged a filthy towel from his back pocket and scrubbed at dirty hands with it. "I thought I had it under control. But the weak spots just gave all at once."

Katherine tried to absorb what Bob was saying. "Weak spots?"

Bob moved closer, his face sorrowful. "Your plumbing, Ms. Tipton. It's gone."

Hysteria bubbled at the back of Katherine's throat. "How could the plumbing be gone?"

"Everything blew," Bob replied, turning the rag over and over in his hands. "Every line has a break."

Dizzy, Katherine sagged against the

porch railing. “I thought you had the water off.”

“I did.” Bob swiped his forehead with his shirtsleeve. “When I finished with the master bath, I turned it back on. The water pressure was just too much.”

Katherine groaned, her body leaning toward Steve on its own. Some devious part of her mind thought he might curve his arm around to comfort her. Instead he patted her between the shoulder blades like a cocker spaniel, and Katherine felt ridiculously outraged.

Steve was finally being decorously impersonal — exactly as he ought. That should please her; after all, if he didn’t make advances, she wouldn’t have to hurt him by rebuffing him. Good Lord, why couldn’t she figure out what she really wanted?

Her mother seemed in no quandary over her desires — she wanted to mow down Bob. Grace accelerated down the stairs and with a huff and a toss of her head, rounded on the man. “You’ll fix Katherine’s plumbing,” Grace demanded, “and you’ll fix it right now.”

Bob met her toe-to-toe. “There’s nothing left to fix. She needs a complete repipe.”

Puffed up with indignation, Grace shook her finger at Bob. "You should have hired real plumbers to do that in the first place."

Bob's face reddened to an alarming shade, and he gurgled something unintelligible. He swallowed once or twice, Adam's apple bouncing.

Intent on forestalling World War III, Katherine hurried down the stairs toward the two combatants. "Excuse me, pardon me," she called out, shoving between them. Behind her, Steve tugged at Bob's arm to pull him back. Katherine pointed to the porch. "Mother, to your corner."

Grace harrumphed, then stomped back up the stairs. Steve threw a companionable arm around Bob's shoulders. "When can you start the repipe?" he asked.

Katherine knew she wouldn't like the answer from the look on Bob's face. "I don't have the supplies on hand to start today," he hedged. "Or the time. I had only today to spare."

"Then start tomorrow!" Grace ordered from the porch.

Shock widened Bob's eyes. "On a Sunday?" he gasped.

"And why not?" Grace leaned over the railing. "It was your incompetence that caused the problem. If you'd repiped in the first place —"

"Mother!" Katherine scolded. "I'm the one that told him not to repipe. I was trying to save money, remember?" She forced a smile on her face. "Monday, Bob?"

"I start work at the big Sundale development Monday," he reminded her.

Katherine covered her eyes with her hand. That was why he was here on a Saturday. It'd be at least a week before he'd be done at Sundale.

But he'd assured Katherine he could do the bathroom in a day. And would've, if her plumbing hadn't been shot to begin with.

She took a calming breath. "Do you know someone else I could call?"

Grace snapped out, "Someone who knows what they're doing, for a change."

Katherine hissed a warning to her mother, then smiled placatingly at Bob. Bob rubbed at his chin. "Most of the local fellas will be at Sundale. I can give you the names of a few guys down in Sacramento."

"I wouldn't trust anyone recommended by that idiot," Grace issued from the front porch.

"Mother!" Katherine chided. She turned to Steve. "You wouldn't have a plumber tucked away in that house of yours, would you?"

Steve cocked a smile at her. " 'Fraid not." He shrugged. "I wish I could be more help."

"You can," Katherine said, leaning close to him. "Would you take my mother down to Java Town and get her a latté?" She flicked a glance at the agitated Grace, then whispered, "Better make it decaf."

Steve shepherded Grace to his car, winking at Katherine as he passed. "I'll drop Cora at home on the way." He pulled out his keys and held them out to the older woman. "Want to drive?"

To Katherine's surprise, her mother took the keys. Grace sped away with a squeal of tires that would have made any teenager proud, and Corazon waved good-bye from the side window.

Bemused, Katherine returned her attention to Bob, laying a hand on his shoulder to urge him into the house. "Let's make those calls now."

At the top of the porch stairs, she snagged the coat hanger, then slipped off her sneakers and socks and slogged into the entryway. Bob followed with his already wet workboots.

"Don't worry about the cleanup, Ms.

Tipton," Bob told her as they made their way to the phone. "I've got my boys on the way right now with a pump."

Katherine picked up her portable phone from the kitchen table and turned it on. She waited for the dial tone. Nothing.

"Oh, by the way," Bob added. "I turned off the electricity. Just as a precaution until we get the mess cleaned up."

Katherine set down the portable with exaggerated care. It wouldn't look good if she snapped it in two. "I'll have to use the upstairs phone," she said as she headed for the stairs.

"Just a minute," Bob called, pulling a worn wallet from a pocket. He fished out several dog-eared business cards. "Here you go. The boys are here — I'll get them started on the cleanup."

After she hung up her clothes and dried her feet, she curled up on the bed to make her calls. Fifteen minutes later, she slumped on the bed in discouragement.

Of the six phone numbers Bob had given her, two had been disconnected, three told her it was too far to travel, and one simply laughed at her when she asked if he could fit her in next week. She stared at the receiver when the last one hung up on her, wondering if she could send a curse through the phone wires.

Then with a groan she bent to drag the Sacramento yellow pages from under her nightstand. Dumping the three-inch-thick doorstop on the bed, she flipped through the flimsy pages until she found the entry for *Plumbing*. Without hope, she began to dial.

Steve gripped the paper latté cup a little tighter as Grace made the turn onto her daughter's cul-de-sac. Whipping around the court, Grace cleared by millimeters the nondescript American sedan parked behind the contractor's truck, then pulled in behind Katherine's BMW with a stomp of brakes. Steve waited for the coffee to stop sloshing, then opened his door with a shaking hand.

Hurrying around the rear of the Mustang on rubbery legs, he handed Grace her latté and retrieved his keys. Grace smiled up at him, a look of genuine happiness on her face. "Thank you," she said, "that was invigorating."

Steve grinned in return. "You're welcome, Mrs. Tipton. You can do wheelies in my Mustang anytime."

She tittered at that, the flush in her cheeks reminding him of her daughter. He vowed anew that he damn well wouldn't let Katherine's sudden coolness defeat him. He'd mulled things over at Java Town, and realized she'd reacted out of fear, fear of the intense emotions between them. They'd only known each other for a few days, after all. She needed a little more time, to accept what they felt for each other. Then she'd forget she was ever engaged to what's-his-name.

Grace's voice jolted him out of his reverie. "Alan! What a nice surprise."

Steve took one look at the fair-haired accountant on Katherine's front porch and growled inwardly. *Very nice,* Steve thought. *Now go home.*

Alan descended the steps and thrust his hand out to Steve. "Walker — what brings you here?"

Your fiancée took her clothes off at my place the other night. I'm just returning them. Steve grinned as he pumped the accountant's hand. "I was in the neighborhood. Thought I'd drop by."

Alan gave Steve's shoulder a hearty slap. "Thanks again for giving Katherine a ride home from the Chamber meeting."

A car horn sounded from the street and Steve turned to see a cross-looking blond woman standing by the car Grace had nearly clipped. "I'll be right there," Alan shouted, waving at her impatiently. Tossing her head, the woman dropped into the passenger seat and slammed the door.

Steve gazed thoughtfully at the woman sitting ramrod-straight in the car. "Does Katherine know you tool around with blondes on the weekend?"

One foot on the porch step, Alan jolted to a stop. "Blondes?" He looked puzzled a moment, then his face cleared. "Oh, her. That's just my secretary, Ms. Beeker."

One look at Ms. Beeker's furtive glances at Alan told Steve the blond woman aspired to be more than Alan's secretary. Steve tucked that interesting tidbit away as he headed up the stairs past Alan.

Steve kicked off his sneakers and socks. "Come on inside," he told Alan. He waited while Grace slipped off her flats, then placed a steadying hand on the older woman's elbow to escort her through the flood.

Alan followed, apparently unperturbed that another man had invited him into his fiancée's home. He seemed more concerned with keeping his loafers dry as he navigated the ponds and lakes of Katherine's house.

"Where's my girl?" he called out.

Steve'd seen Katherine's reaction to that patronizing term; Alan's use of it made Steve want to thump him. "She's upstairs," Steve said. "She'll be down in a minute."

Tiptoeing into the kitchen, Alan spotted the contractor, on his knees monitoring the pump. "Hello, Bob," Alan called out jovially. Bob glanced at Alan, then hunched over the pump, as if he hoped he wouldn't be noticed. Alan pressed on, "Hey, did I miss your call yesterday? I expected to hear from you about that problem with your receivables —"

"Got busy yesterday," Bob mumbled as he tapped the pump with his crescent wrench. He shuffled around so that his back was to Alan.

Bob's obvious rejection didn't seem to faze Alan. The accountant fixed a supercilious smile on his face as he surveyed the chaos in the kitchen.

"For the life of me, I can't understand why she's putting all this energy and her hard-earned money into this ugly old house," he pronounced.

Steve contemplated the nice fat puddle behind Alan, calculating that a well-placed nudge would tip the accountant's behind squarely into it. Steve took a step closer.

"The house is important to her, that's why," Grace sniffed, her surprising defense forestalling Steve's treachery.

"But we've agreed we'll be living at my condo when we're married," Alan barreled on, oblivious to Grace's censure.

"Have you?" Steve would have bet all of last year's profit from HeartStar that Katherine had agreed to no such thing. "Maybe she just wants to finish what she's started."

"But why put so much work into something she won't use?" Alan persisted.

"Why indeed?" Grace said dryly. She looked Alan up and down, as if seeing something she'd never noticed before. "I'll go see what's keeping my daughter," she said, heading for the stairs.

After Grace had gone, Steve turned to Alan. "So what brings you here?"

Alan started to place a hand on the counter, then drew it back, probably because the grout wasn't clean. "The phone here was busy so I came by to tell Katherine I'll be gone a couple days. I'm headed up to Reno."

Pure devilishness exploded inside Steve at the golden opportunity the accountant had unwittingly given him. Leaning close to Alan, he said in a low, confidential tone, "You're going to Reno with Ms. Beeker?"

Alan blinked. "Well, yes. We're attending an accountancy conference together."

"Does Katherine" — Steve gestured with his head upstairs — "know you're going off to Reno with your secretary?"

Alan's mouth hung open a moment, then his cheeks suffused with red. "What are you suggesting?"

Steve waggled his brow lecherously. "Nothing you haven't already thought of, I'm sure."

"But — but —" Alan's mouth flapped as his eyes roved the room looking for answers. "You've got this all wrong."

"Of course I do," Steve said, nodding his head in exaggerated agreement. He heard a snicker from Bob, still hunched over the pump. In a stage whisper, Steve told Alan, "Don't worry. I wouldn't dream of telling Katherine."

"But I . . . I . . ." Alan shoved his hands into the pockets of his neat slacks, then pulled them out. "Ms. Beeker is only joining me in a professional capacity."

"Right." Steve drew out the word as he gave the accountant a broad wink. "Sure. And that's what we tell Katherine. Don't we, Bob?"

Another snigger from the floor, and Alan's face flushed a deeper red. "I don't appreciate your insinuations," he blustered.

"Hey, we understand," Steve assured him, a friendly hand on his arm. "Working together in close quarters, an attractive woman like Ms. Beeker . . ."

"Attractive?" Alan seemed astounded by the notion. "Ms. Beeker?"

"A real looker," Steve affirmed.

Steve could see the wheels of speculation turning within Alan, struggling for purchase. "Ms. Beeker?" he murmured, to himself now. "A looker?"

Good God, Steve thought, hiding a smile. It seemed his attempt to needle the accountant had set in motion entirely new, devishly useful possibilities.

"What do you say we sit down?" Steve said to Alan, sauntering to the breakfast table and scooting up onto it.

But Alan remained standing, shifting from foot to foot, the light of revelation growing in his face. Steve leaned his palms back on the table, well pleased with his machinations. His gratification increased with the arrival of Katherine and Grace.

"No luck," Katherine said as she padded into the kitchen.

When Alan registered her presence, he nearly hopped out of his loafers. He recovered quickly, exclaiming, "Katie!" as he tiptoed through the puddles toward her. Throwing his arms around her, he squeezed her awkwardly and pecked her on the cheek. "I'm so sorry about the mess."

"It certainly isn't your fault," she said, extricating herself from Alan's grip. The alacrity with which she did so heartened Steve.

"Couldn't find anyone?" he asked as he pulled two kitchen stools out for her and Grace.

She waited for her mother to sit before she sank onto the stool, her knees temptingly near his. "There's not a plumber to be had between here and Sacramento," she said.

Steve gazed down at her bare toes curled around the rungs of the stool. He resisted the urge to caress the tops of her feet with the soles of his. "Bob's suggestions didn't pan out?"

She shook her head. "I went through every listing in the phone book, too." She turned to the accountant. "Do you know anyone, Alan?"

"Know anyone?" Alan muttered as he stared at Katherine. Steve could swear he was making comparisons between her and a certain blond secretary.

"A plumber," Katherine said, an edge to her voice.

"No." Alan shook his head as if to dislodge the images dancing there. "No I don't, Katie dear."

Katherine scrutinized Alan a moment, as if trying to puzzle out what was wrong. He wouldn't meet her eye, seeming to find the scars on her linoleum far more interesting.

Her brow furrowed, then she pivoted on her stool to face the plumber. "Bob? I've been wondering . . ."

"What's that, Ms. Tipton?" The stocky man rose to his feet, wiping his hands on his low slung jeans.

Katherine leaned on the breakfast bar, revealing a tantalizing swath of bare skin where her sweatshirt rode up. "Once you've finished cleaning up, can I get by until next week?"

Bob paused in wiping his hands. "Get by?"

"With staying here." She shifted as she spoke, and it was all Steve could do to keep from tracing that sliver of silky skin with his fingertip. "Until you can do the repipe."

Bob stepped closer to the breakfast bar. "Ms. Tipton, you have no water."

Katherine sat up straight, and the hem of her sweatshirt dropped, covering her again. "Couldn't I bring water in?" she asked Bob. "Take sponge baths, that sort of thing?"

Steve entertained a sudden, vivid image of Katherine in the tub and him drizzling a sponge over her body, squeezing a stream of water over her shoulders, down her slim back, stroking along her breasts . . .

Bob's voice intruded on his fantasy. "Ms. Tipton, you have no *toilet*."

Katherine sighed, shoulders dropping in discouragement. "There must be a way."

"There is," Grace said, hopping to her feet. "You'll simply have to stay with me."

Katherine spun toward her mother so abruptly, Steve had to put out a supporting hand to keep her from falling off her stool. "I don't think —"

"You'll sleep on the sofa," Grace continued as if Katherine hadn't spoken.

Katherine tried again. "Mother, I don't —"

"Of course you'll have to alter your routine a bit," Grace steamrollered on. "Get up later — you know what a light sleeper I am."

"But Mother, I —"

"I'm sure we'll get along fine."

"Mother!" Katherine took a breath. "No thank you, Mother."

"But —"

"No."

Grace gazed at her daughter a moment more, then looked away. Keeping her eyes averted, she stepped around Katherine. "It's time for me to go home."

Katherine rose. "Let me walk you to your car."

Grace flung a dismissive hand toward Katherine. "No need. Please let me know where you end up."

Back straight, Grace marched out the door. Katherine watched her go, uncertainty in her face.

Steve gave her shoulder a squeeze. "She'll recover."

"I suppose." She seemed to lean into his caress a moment before she pulled away. "It really would be best for me to stay with Alan."

A shotgun would have had less effect on the daydreaming accountant. "Stay?" he gasped out. "With me?"

"Yes," Katherine responded, a bit impatiently. "In your guest room."

"Oh, well," he began, then gaped at her as the silence stretched. Finally, his brain seemed to kick-start. "Actually, I came by to tell you — I'm going to Reno." He flicked a glance at Steve. "Accountants' conference. I'll be back Wednesday."

"That'll work out fine then," Katherine said. "I'll stay at your place while you're gone."

Alan froze as visions of Ms. Beeker surely pranced in his head. Seizing the opportunity, Steve leaped to his feet and hustled Alan off to the other side of the kitchen. "Not a good idea," he whispered in Alan's ear.

Alan's eyes widened. "Why not?"

Steve took a long look at Katherine, who simmered with a mix of confusion and irritation. "I don't want to tell you your business, but if she were to find . . ." Steve tipped his head in the general direction of the street, where Ms. Beeker waited. ". . . evidence, things might get a bit sticky."

"But there isn't any 'evidence,' " Alan protested.

"Of course not, of course not." Steve gave Alan's shoulder a manly slap. "But sometimes a woman can get upset over the most innocent items."

The accountant stilled, no doubt calculating what might be lying around that could be misconstrued. "It's true Ms. Beeker has visited my condo upon occasion. Strictly in a business capacity, you understand," he added hastily.

Steve sucked in a breath through his teeth. "Risky. If Katherine were to see something that didn't belong —"

"But she wouldn't." Alan clutched at his arm. "She's never been to my place, so she'd never know —"

"Wait," Steve said, stopping Alan's flow of words. "Katherine's never been to your condo?"

"Well, no," the accountant said. "Because of my allergies. That scent she wears always seems to kick them up —"

"Something tells me you're not allergic to Ms. Beeker." Steve didn't wait for Alan's answer. A suspicion had bubbled up in the back of his mind, and he strode across the kitchen to Katherine.

He took her by the shoulders, backed her even farther from her almost-fiancé. "He says you've never been to his place before," he said softly. Katherine shook her head. "And I don't suppose Mr. Fussy has spent much time here."

Her lips tightened. "He's been here once or twice."

Steve swallowed, torn between desperation to know the truth and fear that he was wrong. "But where do you . . . I mean, when do you . . ."

Katherine flushed twelve shades of scarlet. "We don't," she whispered. "We haven't."

Joy fountained up inside Steve at her confirmation. "You haven't? You've never?"

She shook her head again. "We've been waiting."

Steve grinned and turned back to Alan. "Katherine doesn't need to stay at your place after all."

Wary relief blossomed in Alan's eyes. "She doesn't?"

"No." Steve's grin widened. "Because she's staying with me."

Chapter 7

Stay with Steve? The suggestion caused a riot of emotions in Katherine — outrage, indignation . . . sheer excitement.

It was a terrible idea. Entirely inappropriate. And yet . . .

Before her mind could take hold of the tantalizing possibilities, Katherine shook her head. "No," she said. "I can't stay with you."

"Of course you can," Steve said. "My garage apartment's empty and you need a place to stay." He strode across the kitchen to Alan and laid an arm around her almost-fiancé's shoulder. "A perfect solution, wouldn't you say?" he asked Alan.

"I don't know," Alan said uncertainly. He tried to step away from the arm confining him, but Steve just moved with him.

"Allergies can be pretty dicey things," Steve said, guiding Alan to the front door. "Who knows what would happen if Katherine stayed at your place. All her things lying around — that scent — could trigger an episode of anaphylactic shock." He rambled on, playing to Alan's obvious hypochondria.

Alan dug in his heels before Steve could commandeer him outside. "But how would it look if she stayed with you?" He craned his neck around at Katherine. "Maybe —"

Steve hissed what sounded like a warning, and that peculiar guilty look that had flitted across Alan's face earlier took hold again. "Ixnay on the aybe-may," Steve told him under his breath as he bobbed his head toward the open front door. Alan's mouth snapped shut.

Katherine narrowed her gaze on Steve, whose innocent look had trouble written all over it. She moved to her almost-fiancé's side. "Would it bother you if I —"

Alan jumped as if goosed. "Hey!" he said crossly, trying again to tug away from Steve.

"Alan won't mind," Steve answered for him.

"But Alan," Katherine began, then realized she spoke to empty air. Steve had already hustled her almost-fiancé out the door and down the porch steps. "Now wait just a minute," she called out as she followed them down the walk.

Steve didn't even hesitate as he urged Alan to his nondescript sedan. Hurrying to catch up, it took Katherine a moment to recognize the woman sitting inside the car.

Katherine turned to Alan. "What is Ms. Beeker doing here?"

His hand froze on the door handle, his pale blue eyes nearly goggling out of his head. "We . . . we're . . . driving up to the conference together. She's attending the uh, office-management workshops."

A dispassionate part of Katherine's brain signaled her that she probably ought to be jealous. But she couldn't seem to generate even a tickle of that emotion. "Oh," she said calmly. "Then I suppose you'd better go."

"Right, yes," Alan said, fumbling with the door handle. He half lowered himself into the car, then vaulted out again to hurry back over to her. He planted a kiss on her cheek, tossed off a "Bye!", then sprinted back to the car.

Katherine watched Alan and Ms. Beeker pull away from the curb, then turned to Steve. "I'd better call my mother," she said with a sigh.

He rested a hand on the small of her back, nudging her back toward the house. "You ought to let her cool off before you apologize."

Katherine halted at the foot of the porch

steps. "But I have to tell her I've changed my mind — that I'll stay with her after all."

He pressed his palm against her back and her feet ascended the stairs of their own accord. "You're staying with me."

She shook her head. "You're the parent of one of my students. It simply wouldn't look right."

"I'm not suggesting anything out of line." His hand began moving up her spine as they entered the kitchen, leaving sensation in its wake. "The apartment is entirely separate from the house. When my sister Renee stays there, we never even see each other. Unless we want to."

She couldn't find any error in his logic; it sounded like the perfect solution. She could feel herself giving in. "You'd have to let me pay you something."

She knew he wanted to refuse. His eyes sharpened; she could all but see the refusal on his lips. She realized this might provide her the perfect excuse to turn down his offer — if he insisted she stay without payment, she would simply stand her ground and —

His face relaxed into a smile. "We can set a price later."

Why did his unexpected surrender make

her feel so neatly trapped? "It's settled then," she said slowly. "I'll get some things together, meet you at your place."

His place. A shiver trembled up her spine at the intimate sound of the words.

"Tell you what," he said, checking his watch. "Give me an hour. I need to check the place, make sure it's stocked."

"An hour," she repeated, feeling shell-shocked. "Sure."

"Great." He stroked her back one last time, then let his fingers drift across her shoulders and down her arm. "See you later."

For a moment after he'd gone, Katherine hugged her arm tight to herself, enjoying the lingering heat. How, she mused, could such a simple gesture start such a fire in her? She shook her arm, as if to shake off the aftereffects of his touch. But the sensation curled deliciously in the center of her.

"I'm done, Ms. Tipton."

She nearly shrieked at the sound of Bob's voice. She'd entirely forgotten he was there. "Oh, good," she managed over the thundering of her heart.

He backed out from under the sink. "And if someone else can do the repipe before Monday, I won't mind a bit."

"I'll let you know if I find someone," she promised.

"Fine," he said, as he crouched to gather up his equipment. He dawdled over the job, placing each wrench in his toolbox with care. "You know, Ms. Tipton . . ."

Katherine leaned against the kitchen counter. "What's that, Bob?"

The contractor snapped shut the lid on the red-metal box. "That Mr. Walker's a pretty nice fellow."

Katherine stiffened as she stared down at the heavyset man. "I'm engaged, Bob."

Bob wouldn't look at her. "I know, but . . ." Katherine wondered if he considered Alan a "pretty nice fellow." Somehow she didn't think so.

"And not to Mr. Walker," she added, a bit more firmly.

He sighed as he pulled himself to his feet. "I'd better be getting home."

Katherine watched him go, then headed upstairs, troubled more by what Bob didn't say than by what he did say. It seemed as if everyone knew exactly how she should run her personal life. That might have irritated her more if she didn't feel so uncertain about it herself.

An hour later, with her house locked up and a week's worth of clothes packed in the trunk of her BMW, she drove to Steve's. A sense of homecoming washed over her as she pulled up to his house. The sun lay low on the horizon, its dying brilliance tinting the sky with vermilion. Lights glowed inside the house, and the scent of a wood fire filled the air.

Just as she reached his porch steps, the door opened and Steve hurried out to help her with her suitcase. He'd showered; his thick hair curled in damp waves and his skin radiated a tantalizing spicy scent. He'd changed, too, into a cable-knit oatmeal-colored sweater and gray slacks.

"Are you going out?" she asked as he led her around the side of the house toward the garage. "I mean it's none of my business, but I wondered —"

"No, I'm not going out." He led the way up a flight of narrow steps beside the garage. "Dad's cooking tonight. He wanted me to ask you to join us."

Say no, her mind told her. "I'd love to," she said.

"Great." He reached the small landing at the top of the stairs and pushed the door to the garage apartment open, then stepped back to let her go in first. Katherine brushed against him in the small space, allowing herself the luxury of enjoying the brief contact.

Steve followed her inside. He flipped on the light, chasing the shadows from the room. The door opened into the tiny kitchen. Katherine's eyes skidded from the kitchen's orange-painted cupboards, to the lemon yellow curtains, to the gold-flecked Formica covering the counters. A woodtone dinette table with two chrome-and-vinyl chairs dominated one corner.

The scarred pale green linoleum of the kitchen led into the rust-colored hi-lo carpet of the living area. Purple-striped wallpaper and an eclectic mix of furniture competed for attention in the room. Mismatched ersatz Early American end tables were placed next to a worn black vinyl lounger, which sat kitty-corner to an oversize sofa in a truly hideous green-and-rust plaid.

Steve must have seen the dismay on her face, because he said, "It's clean. That's about all I can say for it."

"It's . . . it's . . ." Katherine searched for something nice to say about the apartment. Then she glimpsed the humor dancing in Steve's eyes, and she burst out laughing. "It's amazingly ugly. Absolutely awful."

Laughing with her, Steve dropped her

suitcase in front of a minuscule closet in one corner of the living room. "Believe it or not, my sister loves it this way. Everything in here is a garage-sale find."

"I never would have guessed," Katherine managed, then she burst into another fit of giggles.

"Bathroom's in there." Steve pointed to a doorway thickly curtained with red-and-green plastic beads. "The sofa opens out into a bed. Clean sheets, but lumpy mattress, I'm afraid."

"Of course." Katherine wiped away tears of laughter and scanned the garish room again. "This place could give me nightmares."

"If it does," he gestured out the window with its thick ruffle of blood-red velvet drapes, "my room is there. Just flash your light, and I'll come running."

"To my rescue?" she murmured, surprised at the throaty sound of her voice.

His gaze was meltingly warm. "Always," he said softly in response.

The promise, the invitation in his eyes drew her; she knew she could step right over the edge and be engulfed. Instead she turned away. "What time's dinner?" she asked.

He hesitated long enough for her to look

back up at him. The fire was still there. "In about an hour," he said softly. His gaze remained steady on her. "Just come in the back."

Katherine nodded and moved to her suitcase. "See you then," she said as she knelt to open it.

Silence, then the sound of his shoes scraping on the floor and his footsteps hurrying down the stairs. Katherine sank to the floor, hugging her knees to her chest.

She sat that way a long time, aching for the loss of something she couldn't name.

She'd regained her equanimity an hour later, snug in a thick purple chenille sweater and ice-cream white leggings as she walked across the yard in the October chill. By the time she got to the back door, the cold had penetrated her sweater, and she pushed open the door, eager to get back inside.

Warmth enveloped her when she stepped into the utility room of the main house, and she felt more than physical comfort. This was like coming indoors just after dusk, when the last moment of play had been squeezed out of the day, and her mother was there with a smile and a cup of hot chocolate.

She paused by the washing machine, hand on the cool metal surface. That memory had to be wrong, an embellishment on reality. But the image returned — Katherine's small, cold hands taking the hot cup from her mother, her mother's soft, genuine smile, the smell of cocoa rising from the cup.

Her childhood picture of her mother had always been of a cold, hard woman. Yet when she thought back, Katherine realized that although Grace had often been stiffly formal and bossy to boot, there'd always been a soft center of love inside her.

Something released within Katherine, a tightness she hadn't even known had been there. Her exasperating, impossible mother *did* love her — had always — and for the first time Katherine understood that in her heart instead of just in her head.

Grinning like the child she remembered, Katherine prompted her feet to move and headed through the pantry toward the kitchen. At the exact moment she pushed aside the half-open pocket door, Steve's father burst through from the other side, all frantic energy.

"Hey! Hello! You must be Katherine! Sorry, can't stop to chat —"

Steve stepped up to steady her as he barreled through the pantry.

"Katherine, I've never formally introduced you to my dad —" But the older man was gone. Katherine leaned into Steve's grasp, let her hands rest on his chest, the nubby knit tickling her palms.

"His name is Ralph."

Katherine tipped her head up to Steve. "Your father seems a bit edgy."

" 'Scuse me, kids," came Ralph's big voice.

They both jumped back, parting as Ralph ran back the other way. Steve laughed, pushing his fingers through his hair. "Apparently he has a guest coming. When I asked him who, he nearly bit my head off."

Katherine stepped into the kitchen, admiring the carved-oak cupboards, some with etched-glass fronts. Intricate tilework covered the counters. Under her feet, hardwood inlay softened with throw rugs stretched from the pantry end of the kitchen to the dining area at the other end.

A dream kitchen, but right now every square inch of counter space, as well as the breakfast table tucked into the corner, was laden with pots, pans, bowls, and cutting boards. The dinner-making mess even littered the heavy claw-footed dining table at the far end of the room.

Ralph jammed a can of water chestnuts into the electric can opener, then swore when he cut his finger on the lid. He glared at Steve and Katherine as he sucked at his finger. "Don't just stand there! Get me a bandage!"

Corazon, who sat wide-eyed on a kitchen stool, hopped up. "I'll get it for you, *abuelito.*" She hurried from the room.

Steve rested a hand on Katherine's shoulder. "I think we'd best leave the disaster area."

As Steve guided her from the room, Katherine heard the sharp sizzle of food in hot oil and the scent of cooking beef. Just as she and Steve reached the bottom of the staircase, Ralph shouted, "Ouch! Damn it! Cora, get me that burn medicine, too!"

Steve laughed, shaking his head, then urged Katherine up the stairs. "I have a new computer game I wanted to show you."

Katherine smiled up at him as they mounted the stairs. "Is he safe in there by himself?"

"Dad's always a catastrophe in the kitchen." They reached the upstairs hall and turned to the left. The sconces lining the hall glowed like gaslight. "It doesn't help that his guest is twenty minutes late."

When they reached Steve's bedroom, Katherine followed so closely, she bumped into him when he paused to flip on the lights. She put out her hands to steady herself, then snatched them away when of their own accord they stroked down his back to his waist.

Katherine folded her arms across her middle, tucking away her recalcitrant hands. "So who's coming to dinner?" Katherine asked casually.

Steve's low chuckle told her he hadn't missed her near downfall. "He wouldn't tell me. A surprise, he said."

As Steve crossed to power up his computer, Katherine delighted anew in the plush comfort of his room. The tall windows revealed the last pink glimmer of sunset fading against the black night. The window seat below invited her to curl up with the patchwork quilt and open book lying there.

As Steve clicked his mouse, Katherine gave in to temptation and moved to the window seat. She sank onto the soft cushions, slipping off her shoes and tucking her feet under the well-worn quilt. Hefting the book, one finger holding Steve's place, she read the title. *Saving the Stumbling Start-*

Up, it said, then in smaller letters underneath, *How to Be a White Knight Without Falling Off Your Horse*. Written in even smaller letters in the lower right-hand corner was the name Steve Walker.

"Here it is," Steve called from the other side of the room.

"You wrote this?" Katherine said, brandishing the book at him.

Not looking up, he typed a string of letters on the keyboard. "Yeah, I did."

"Then you're a writer," she persisted.

"I wrote one book," he said, eyes on the computer monitor. "It might have sold a hundred copies."

"Oh." She carefully laid the book down as she'd found it, feeling deflated. She'd wanted to believe he was a success at something, that he was more than an overgrown teenager living in his father's house, spending all his time playing video games.

Why should it matter to her? Because she cared about him, of course. People were supposed to care about each other, weren't they? It didn't imply any special meaning, that she cared about *him* more than the father of any other student.

Not wanting to pursue that line of thought any further, she padded across the room to sit beside Steve at the computer.

She scrambled for something intelligent to say about the game displayed on the monitor. "Interesting colors," she finally said.

"Actually, they're very unappealing." Eyes focused on the screen, he clicked with the mouse, bringing up a new display. "That's the first thing I'm going to suggest. Color selectability."

"Would they take your suggestion?" Katherine asked. "I mean, does the opinion of a video game tester carry that much weight?"

He laughed, as if very amused by her comment. "Let's just say this particular company is very interested in what I've got to say about its product."

He took her through the game's screens, explaining each one. Finally a light dawned in Katherine. "It's a math game," she said. "The problems are all so jumbled, I didn't get it at first."

"Problem number two," Steve commented. "There's no unifying theme. What it needs is some input from an educational expert."

His hands stilled on the mouse, and, after a beat, he turned to look at her speculatively. "What?" she asked.

A smile spread slowly across his face. He seemed to consider whether to speak.

Then he turned back to the computer. "It'll keep."

While Katherine puzzled over that, he exited the game and powered down the computer. "Shall we go rescue Dad?" he suggested. "His guest must have arrived by now."

Curiosity gnawed at her as they descended the stairs. What had he been about to say? She was certain that it involved her.

Head down, pondering the tantalizing possibilities of what was left unsaid, she didn't notice Steve stopped in his tracks until he put out a hand to stop her. She craned her neck up at him. "What?" He pointed to the dining room.

Cousin Denny dangled from the dining room chandelier, a cast iron relic of a sturdier age, bolted into a ceiling beam. He furrowed his brow in concentration as he swayed, his worn loafers brushing the table with each gentle arc. Grinning with delight from her perch on the kitchen stool, Cora clapped her hands each time Denny dislodged an item from the table.

A study in agitation, Ralph waved a threatening spoon at Denny. "Do your damned experiments another time! I have guests for dinner."

Face clouded with thought, Denny gripped the arms of the chandelier more firmly and lifted his feet higher. The chandelier creaked alarmingly as he swung. "This will only take a minute," he muttered.

"What?" Katherine managed. She took a breath and started again. "What is he doing?"

Steve shook his head slowly. "I have no idea. This is a new one on me."

A puff of plaster dust sifted down, and Katherine cringed. "Can it hold him?"

"Should," Denny said, shifting on the chandelier. "I reinforced the ceiling here when I installed it, and it's bolted into a beam."

Ralph brandished his spoon again. "That was two years ago, you damned idiot. Why test it now?"

Denny's answer was forestalled by the bing-bong of the front doorbell. Cora hopped off her stool. "I'll get it," she sang out as she raced to the front door.

Ralph started tugging at Denny's legs, which only brought down another cloud of dust. Katherine's shriek was drowned by the thundering of feet on the stairs as the twins exploded onto the scene.

"What's for dinner?" they chorused.

Melinda moved toward the electric wok on the kitchen counter, unconcerned with Denny's antics. "Yuk! Beef with snow peas," she squealed.

"I *like* beef with snow peas," Theresa put in.

"*You* like Tim Phillips, too!"

"I do not!"

"Do too!"

"Ms. Tipton, Ms. Tipton," cried Cora from the foyer. "Look who's here!"

Katherine dragged her eyes away from the suspended Denny to see who Cora towed in from the front door. She didn't warrant the first message her brain sent her, figuring the dimmer light from the living room tricked her into seeing things.

She blinked, but the same person still stood there at Cora's side, staring openmouthed up at Denny.

Her mother.

Steve's gaze slipped from mother to daughter, and he wondered who was more aghast than who. He could see Grace struggling to school her face into normalcy, but as more plaster dust frosted Denny's thinning pate, she seemed to give up and grope for someplace to sit.

Steve grasped Grace's arm and tugged

her to the other end of the long room. "Good to see you, Grace." He pulled out a chair from the breakfast table and settled her in it.

"Mother! What are you doing here?" Katherine asked from directly behind him.

Grace kept her eyes on Denny. "What is that man doing?"

"Getting down," Ralph snapped, banging on Denny's knees with his spoon. "Now!"

Denny released his grip and thumped onto the dining-room table. "I was done, anyway," he said, stepping to a chair, then the floor. Muttering to himself, he headed for the stairs.

Ralph stabbed at the air with his spoon. "You'd damn well better dress for dinner!"

Then he turned back to his wok, and the twins resumed their quarrel. Cora, ever the avid observer of life's goings-on, seemed to be taking notes on Melinda and Theresa's spat. Early teenager training, no doubt.

Steve returned his attention to Grace. "You must be Dad's surprise dinner guest."

Grace looked ready to bolt, and Steve figured only her good manners kept her pinned to her chair. She nodded faintly, one hand coming up to pat her impeccable coif. Then her gaze sharpened on Katherine.

"Ralph told me you're staying here."

Katherine's cheeks flushed an appealing pink. "Yes, I am. When did you meet Ralph?"

"Steve introduced us," Grace said primly. "I get to have a love life, too, you know. Looks like yours is definitely picking up."

"Love life?" Katherine blurted, then her hand flew up to cover her mouth. What was her mother talking about?

She avoided Steve's amused gaze, turning back to her mother. "There's nothing wrong with my staying here temporarily. Steve's garage apartment isn't connected to the main house. It's perfectly proper."

Grace sniffed. "You wouldn't stay with your own mother."

She'd surely meant to be censorious, but a trace of hurt wove throughout the words. Katherine must have heard it, too, because her face softened.

"Mom, you know how we are in close quarters. We'd be at each other's throats the whole time." Katherine moved to put an arm across Grace's shoulders. "I love you too much to do that."

"Well," Grace said, reaching up to enfold Katherine's hand in hers. "I love you, too, sweetie."

Katherine's eyes misted with tenderness. She glanced up at Steve, pleased surprise on her face. Steve suspected this was not the usual interaction between mother and daughter. He understood Katherine's reserve a little better now, and felt renewed gratitude for his own mother's constant love.

His father's bark disrupted his musings. "Now that we have that settled, let's set the table."

Melinda and Theresa hurried to clear the dining-room table, as little Cora swiped the table clean of plaster dust with a wet rag. The older girls slapped plates down with brisk, practiced efficiency. Corazon added napkins, then all three laid out the silverware.

"Now sit, everyone," his father ordered, and the girls raced to comply. When Grace would have sat as far from Ralph as possible at the opposite end of the table, his father snatched her sleeve to redirect her. "You're next to me, Gracie."

Cousin Denny returned, the cuffs of his white dress shirt only slightly frayed, his brown slacks only a little baggy at the knees. He sat opposite the twins, leaving two chairs side by side on the end for Steve and Katherine.

When they were all seated, Ralph laid steaming bowls of rice and beef with snow peas on the table. Melinda raced through the blessing, then the serving bowls traveled around the table from hand to hand until everyone had filled their plates.

Holding her chopsticks expertly, Katherine scooped up her first bite. "Delicious," she sighed around the mouthful.

A bit of rice clung to the corner of her mouth, and the pink tip of her tongue flicked out to retrieve it. Steve nearly groaned aloud watching her, aching to trace that moist path with his fingertip.

A wrangle between his father and Denny tugged him out of his momentary erotic fantasy. They'd launched into another round of good-natured insults, each trying to top the other. The twins added to the noise level with a string of knock-knock jokes that sent Corazon into squeals of laughter.

Steve turned to Katherine again, curious to see her reaction to the free-for-all around the table. A tender smile lit her face as she watched Corazon.

Cora caught Katherine looking at her,

and her face brightened in a million-watt grin. Katherine smiled back, her hand over her heart as if to hold in the joy.

Good for you, Steve silently told his daughter. *You hook her, I'll reel her in.*

Succumbing to his temptation to touch her, Steve ran his knuckles along her arm. "Are we all set for the carnival?"

An appealing pink flush colored her cheeks. "C-carnival?" she stuttered.

"The Halloween carnival." Figuring he'd try rattling her brain a bit more, he squeezed her hand. "At the school."

"Oh! Yes." She pulled her hand away and tucked it into her lap. "The parent group assured me everything will be ready for next Saturday."

"Daddy's doing the Haunted House," Cora piped up. "And *abuelito*'s telling scary stories."

Katherine turned her smile on Ralph. "The parent group told me they had someone lined up for the storytelling booth. I didn't know it was you."

"I need a helper, though," his father said, looking around the table. "Someone to keep an eye on the kids." His eyes rested on Denny, on the twins, on Steve and Katherine. On everyone but Grace. "Reassure the ones who seem too frightened."

Steve grinned at his father's masterful ploy. Grace seemed to expand with irritation as she watched Ralph, scooting up taller in her chair as if to flag his attention.

Finally, she blurted out, "*I'll* do it."

Ralph beamed at her. "Why thank you, Grace. I think the witch costume will fit you perfectly."

For a moment, Grace looked as if she didn't know how to take that and Katherine had to squelch her smile. Then the older woman tipped her chin up in determination. "Just tell me where and when, Mr. Walker."

Steve leaned close to Katherine's ear. "I think they actually like each other. This is just preliminary sparring."

Katherine giggled, a captivating sound. "She'll keep your father on his toes, believe me."

The rest of the meal passed amiably, if noisily. The twins squabbled their way through the cleanup while the adults took coffee into the living room. Steve would have sat next to Katherine on the plush leather sofa, but Grace, attempting to put some real estate between herself and Ralph, beat him to it.

Grace dominated the conversation, asking Denny about his days at the

Capitol, fuming at Ralph's smart cracks. Then his father switched gears, his sharp jokes giving way to compliments, praise for her insightful understanding of State politics.

Which caught Grace completely off guard. In awe of his father's savvy, Steve watched Grace melt under Ralph's charm. Would the same approach work on the daughter? Steve wondered.

All the charm in the world would do him no good now, Steve realized when he looked past Grace at Katherine. Her coffee cup nestled in her lap, her head back against the sofa, she slept. Her dark lashes shadowed lacy crescents onto her cheeks, and her lips had parted slightly in relaxation.

Steve wanted nothing more than to gather her into his arms and cuddle her in his lap. She'd be mortified, of course, to wake and find herself there. So he resisted the impulse, contenting himself with gazing at her tranquil face as the conversation rolled around him.

A splash of warm liquid on her hand jarred Katherine awake. Steve stood over her, prying the cup of coffee from her fingers. "Time for bed, I think," he said softly.

Katherine blinked and looked around her. She and Steve were alone in the room. "Where's my mother?" she asked around a yawn.

"Dad's walking her out. You nodded off sometime between the argument about flood control and the heated discussion of fairy shrimp."

Katherine rose, feeling creaky. "I'm sure my mother opposed everything, just on general principle."

"Let's just say they agreed to disagree."

She studied him sleepily.

"What on earth possessed you to introduce them, anyway?"

"Oh, I don't know. Dad's been getting a little withdrawn. Obsessing over small things. I thought Grace might snap him out of it."

Remembering Ralph clipping the lawn with manicure scissors on her first visit to this house, Katherine could only nod in agreement.

Steve draped an arm across her shoulders and walked with her through the kitchen and out the back door. The chill air bit into her, burrowing beneath her sweater.

"I hope the apartment is heated," Katherine muttered as she mounted the stairs.

"We-ell," Steve said, drawing out the word. "There are plenty of blankets."

Katherine turned to him as she pushed open the door. "No heat?"

He shrugged. "My sister likes it that way."

Her brain still muzzy with sleep, she put a hand out on the stair rail to steady herself. "How will I keep warm?"

The question hung like an invitation between them. She should say something to blunt the erotic suggestion, should walk inside and close the door between them.

Katherine took a step inside, eyes locked with Steve's. She fumbled for the light, but his hand caught hers. "Don't," he murmured.

"Why —"

He gestured toward the window with its heavy red-velvet drapes. "They don't close. Half the neighbors could see us."

He shut the door quietly, then moved toward her, giving her every chance to back away. When she held her ground, he stepped close to her and drew his hand across her cheek.

"Katherine . . ."

He whispered her name, a question, a plea, one that begged for response. Suddenly, she ached for him, here in the intimacy of this small room. She tipped her head, fitting herself into his palm, then rubbed against it like a cat.

"I shouldn't . . ." she began, her words a sigh. She turned to let her lips brush across his palm, gloried in his sharp intake of breath. She looked up at him, her eyelids heavy and wanting to close. "What about Alan? I'm engaged to him . . . sort of."

"You don't love him," he rasped, curving his hand around to the back of her neck. He pulled her toward him, his lips a fraction from hers. "You can't marry someone you don't love."

"But I can count on him," she said, then moaned as his lips pressed softly into hers. "He's steady. Dependable. Tried and true."

"Oh, I don't know about that," Steve murmured, then slid his other hand around to the small of her back. He pulled her closer, pressing her into him. He was hard, and her body responded to his readiness, her hips thrusting toward him.

"Good God," he gasped out. "You're making me crazy."

Her arms moved around him of their own accord, her fingers playing across the thick knit of his sweater. His mouth covered hers at last, this time consuming her, his tongue thrusting in, sliding alongside hers, sensation bursting from the contact. Her body seemed to melt in hot waves from her center, and she grabbed up handfuls of his sweater to pull him more tightly to her.

His mouth moved from her lips to her cheek, then her throat, his tongue flicking in a hot, wet trail. When his breath first touched her ear, a soft mew of excitement slipped from her lips. His tongue laved her sensitive lobe, and she thought her knees would give way.

Just this once, she thought dimly. She could let him make love to her just this once. Then she'd know what hot passion felt like. She could live the rest of her life with good old Mr. Dependably Dull if she could only experience this fire before she did the right thing . . . and married the man her mother wanted her to marry.

"God, Katherine," Steve groaned, his words sifting into her ear. "I want to be inside you so badly."

"Yes," she whispered, her hands moving restlessly across his back. She wanted to curl into his warmth, revel in the joy of his climax.

His hands trembled as they glided down to the hem of her sweatshirt and slipped underneath. She arched at the first touch of his fingertips against her bare flesh, then felt herself sway.

His hands slid up, across her ribs, to her breast. She gasped when he brushed against her nipple, felt it harden under the lace of her bra. Sensation jolted from his touch to her center, and an aching warmth pooled between her legs.

"You don't feel this with him," Steve murmured with raw urgency, "do you?"

"No," she said, the word slipping out on a breath.

He moved his palm back and forth across her nipple, until she thought she would scream from the building tension.

His lips brushed against her ear as his hand continued its relentless motion. "Does he touch you like this?" His other hand skimmed down her body, cupped her at the vee of her legs. "Like this?"

A moan started deep in her throat as his fingers began to move against her. Feather-light, they stroked the sensitive flesh, rubbing against the thin knit of her leggings.

Katherine wanted nothing more than to sink to the floor and pull him down with her.

He seemed to sense her desire because he backed toward the sofa, tugging her with him. He pulled her down into his lap, positioning her legs so that she straddled him.

The hard ridge of him pressed between her legs and she rocked her pelvis to feel his length. He groaned, an animal sound, and gripped her hips so fiercely, she thought he'd pull her right inside him.

"I want you, Katherine," he said raggedly. "God, I need you so much."

She thrust against him again, marveling at his rock-hard flesh, at her own wet readiness. "I want you," she whispered. She pushed her doubts aside, willing to endure any regret for this one brilliant moment.

"Katherine." His fingers laced through her hair, his hand curving around the back of her neck to pull her close. "I love you. God, I love you."

Chapter 8

So caught in the haze of erotic passion, the words didn't register at first. Then he thrust against her, tipping her alarmingly close to the edge, wiping out all thought.

"I love you," he said again, this time more insistent. He pulled back, holding her away from him. "Katherine, did you hear me? I said I love you."

It was as if he had slapped her. She could almost feel the sting on her cheek. "No, you don't."

He held her face in two hands. "I do."

She scrambled from his lap, feeling her way across the room to the lights. She slapped them on and whirled to face him. "You can't."

Eyes narrowed against the brightness, Steve rose, readjusting his slacks with a pained expression. He moved toward her, and Katherine knew if he touched her, she might not be able to pull away again. She shook her head, pressing back against the wall.

Eyes never leaving her face, Steve hesitated, then changed course, leaning against the slice of wall between kitchen and living area. "I love you, Katherine," he repeated quietly.

Katherine shook her head again in denial, her hair scattering into her eyes. "You don't."

"You can't change what I feel," he told her. A beat, then he added, "Nor what you feel."

"Oh, no." She flung her hands up to ward off his words. "Don't say it. Don't even think it."

"I will." He advanced on her again, the heat of passion still shimmering in his eyes. "I love you, Katherine," he murmured, drawing closer. "And if you'd be honest —" Closer. "— with yourself, you'd admit —" He stood over her now, head dipped intimately close to her ear. He whispered the words, "You love me, too."

She squeaked free of him, stumbling into the living area. "I don't! I don't love you." She brushed against the ugly plaid sofa, then jerked back as if the heat of their bodies still lingered there. "I couldn't. I hardly know you."

He didn't come after her again, didn't have to; his eyes held her captivated just the same. "You damn well know the accountant, but you don't love him." He laughed, triumph and victory in the sound. "You won't even sleep with him."

Her cheeks burned, and she tucked her arms across her middle. "I told you. We're waiting."

He shook his head. "You're not waiting. You just don't feel anything for him. If you were mine —"

"I suppose you'd be dragging me off to bed!"

"You know damn well I wouldn't have to drag you." He gave her a lazy smile. "But we'd be so hot for each other, we'd have made it legal in Reno long before now."

She wanted to deny what he said, but she knew the truth of it. Steve would never let her put off their marriage as Alan had. Steve would demand that they wed, demand that she go to their bed — and she would, willingly, joyfully leaping into his love and passion.

Oh, God. I do love him.

With a little cry of despair, she turned away from him before he could see the truth in her eyes. "Would you please go," she managed, throwing the words over her shoulder.

She sensed that he took a step toward her. "Katherine."

"Go," she said more emphatically. "Or

I'll pack up my things and find another place to stay."

For a moment, she heard nothing but his breathing, the sound controlled as if he held back anger. Then footsteps thumped across the floor, truncating with the slam of the door. After a pause, they started down the stairs again.

Moving with exaggerated care, as if a thoughtless motion might cause her to fly apart, she got ready for bed. Teeth brushed, face washed, pajamas donned, she tugged the cushions from the sofa bed, trying not to think about what she and Steve had done there earlier.

It was only when the lights were off and she curled in a tight ball in the middle of the lumpy bed that she let go. The tears came quietly at first, then with loud sobs, all of the emotion pouring out into the pillow.

She loved him. Not Alan, the dependable accountant. But Steve, the flaky video game player with no visible means of support and a family so crazy they seem to have sprung from a video game themselves.

She loved Steve. Life couldn't get much worse.

"Ms. Tipton!"

Katherine could barely make out the sound of her name over the roar of Halloween revelers in the school gym. Scanning the orderly chaos, she caught sight of Mrs. Williams barreling toward her.

Tugging up the pants of her skunk costume, she pasted a carnival-happy smile on her face. "What's up?" she asked the frazzled parent.

Mrs. Williams ran her fingers through her choppy blond hair in agitation. "We're out of coffee. I thought we had enough, but —"

"No problem," Katherine told her. Gathering up the skunk's tail that threatened to tangle with her legs, she led Mrs. Williams through the throng of children toward the exit. "There's some in the teachers' lounge. We'll replace it later."

As Mrs. Williams sprinted across the yard toward the lounge, Katherine sagged against the doorjamb. Her emotions had been all over the place since last Saturday, swinging from despair to elation back to despair. Each time her heart would remember her love for Steve, it would sing, then drag itself down at the impossibility of the situation.

She'd realized she had to keep well clear

of him for the sake of her sanity. From Sunday, when he showed up on her doorstep to invite her to breakfast, until now, she'd danced an intricate sidestep, contriving ruses and improbable excuses to keep herself away from him. She left for school each day as early as she could and stayed as long as her energy would hold out.

The fact that Alan had been busy every night this week hadn't helped. Just when she could have used the distraction of her almost-fiancé, he seemed to be buried under an extraordinary amount of work for the tax off-season.

As she gazed around her at the costumed children racing madly from one attraction to the next, she felt numb with exhaustion. Thank God Steve's domain, the Haunted House, was clear on the other side of the schoolyard. With any luck, she might avoid seeing him at all tonight.

She strolled the perimeter of the gym, checking the status of each booth. A long line of customers waited at the cotton-candy machine, each impatient for their own paper cone of the sticky sweet. Several parents loitered around the mulled cider station, sipping fragrant cups of what the Student Council had whimsically named "witches' brew."

Children clutching fistfuls of tickets won at the carnival games, packed the prize booth. Two harried parents rushed from side to side of the booth, trying to fill prize requests as quickly as possible. Katherine stepped in, ordering the children into two lines, informing them that anyone who took cuts would be banished to last place.

After assigning a roving parent to police the lines, she continued her patrol of the gym. Mr. Hinkins at the Pumpkin Toss needed help fishing a beanbag from the retracted basketball hoop; Katherine tracked down the custodian to have the hoop lowered. Mrs. Lacey at the Wizard's Walk needed a bathroom break; Katherine stood in for her until she returned.

Satisfied that all was well in the gym, Katherine wandered over to the nearby classroom where the storyteller presided. After the brightness of the gym, it took her a moment to adjust her eyes to the dim light of the storytelling room.

Steve's father, in a floor-length purple robe sparked with silver stars and crescent moons, paced the front of the classroom as he intoned his stories. The children sat wide-eyed on the floor where the desks had been pushed aside. Ralph occasionally thumped a carved wooden staff on the floor for emphasis, the noise startling the children each time.

Her mother, in a black witch's hat and dress, hovered on the sidelines. Grace kept a watchful eye on the crowd of children, apparently gauging their fearfulness. At one point, she glided over to a little boy just beginning to crumple in tears, and urged the child toward the door.

Katherine stepped outside with her mother. She watched Grace gently wipe tears from the boy's face, then made sure he knew where to find his parents before he raced off.

"They're so wonderful," Grace said softly as she watched the boy scoot into the gym.

"Most of the time," Katherine said wryly, then she smiled at her mother. "Now why is it you've never come to help in the school before?"

Grace looked at her in surprise. "You've never asked me."

"You're right. I guess it never occurred to me that you'd want to."

Grace laughed. "I don't know that it ever occurred to me, either."

"Then consider yourself asked. I'd love to have you here."

The glow on her mother's face seemed

to make the heaviness in Katherine's heart grow in weight, making her loneliness even harder to bear. She turned away, gazed across the moon-brightened schoolyard.

Grace touched her arm. "What is it?"

Once she might have put her mother off, but now, with their growing closeness, she couldn't. "I don't know what I want, Mom," she said with a sigh. Then she surprised them both when she asked her mother, "Did you love Daddy when you married him?"

Grace considered the question carefully before replying. "I loved your father very much," she said softly. "I think too much sometimes."

"Why?" Katherine implored her mother, desperate for an answer. "Why too much?"

Grace's eyes were troubled. "Because I forgave him too easily. When he made me angry, I let the love wash it away. And he couldn't hold on to money. It just seemed to go through his fingers somehow. Having to do without so much, well, maybe it made me tougher. I raised you to value qualities like dependability — and hard work. I wanted you to have the security in life I couldn't give you."

Grace sighed. "I was never able to put

much aside. Or give you the little luxuries you wanted."

Katherine sighed, too, remembering the bad old days of digging for change in the sofa cushions. "Daddy didn't leave you much, did he?"

"The old house. The life insurance." She shrugged. "Enough to get you and your sister through college."

They stood silent for a long moment, listening to the wind blow their regrets and reminiscences across the schoolyard. Then Grace turned to Katherine, her gaze sharp. "Why this sudden interest in whether I loved your father?"

Katherine looked away, not wanting her mother to see the doubt on her face. But her mother's shrewd eyes caught it anyway.

"Katherine," Grace prodded. When Katherine still would not turn toward her, she said in a more imperious tone, "Katherine Elizabeth!"

Katherine looked at her sidelong. "What?"

"You don't love him, do you?" she asked. "Alan, I mean."

Woeful, Katherine could only shake her head. Grace huffed and planted her hands on her hips. "Then you break off the engagement, Katherine Elizabeth. I won't have you marrying someone you don't love."

Katherine's despair seemed to tighten around her. "But he makes me feel secure, Mama," she wailed.

"Security isn't more important than love, Katherine," Grace said, wagging a finger at her.

"It is when the one you love is a total flake," Katherine insisted. "You married someone like that and look how unhappy —"

"Hold on there," her mother said, putting up a hand to stop her daughter's tirade. "Back up. What did you say about the one you love?"

Katherine could have bitten off her tongue. "I was speaking hypothetically," she said, the words unconvincing even to her.

Grace looked at her sharply. "You aren't unhappy because you don't love Alan. You're unhappy because you *do* love . . . Steve Walker?"

Katherine shook her head vehemently. "I don't. I can't. I want certainty in my life, not the craziness we had with Daddy."

"But it wasn't all crazy, sweetheart." Grace's eyes softened. "There was love there. At least in the beginning. Before I got so scared. And so angry with him."

Katherine wanted to deny it, to refuse to remember that there were good times. But that would have been a lie. "Mama, I know there was love. I did love Daddy, but I never felt like I could . . ."

"Count on him?" Grace asked, a whisper of steel in her tone. "With him bouncing from one so-called surefire investment to another so that we never knew if we could pay the bills?"

Katherine nodded, still aching at the memory. "Alan's speeches may put me to sleep, Mama, and I may not feel anything when he touches me —"

"Like with Steve?" Grace put in.

Heat rose in her cheeks. "Yes." She faced her mother. "But I can count on Alan, Mama. As crass as it sounds, I know he's going to bring in a paycheck every week."

Grace blinked at Katherine's insistent tone. "But Katherine, why would you think Steve couldn't do the same?"

"Mom, Alan owns a successful accounting firm. Steve makes a living playing computer games —"

Her expression puzzled, Grace said slowly, "I suppose owning a computer-game company isn't as traditional as accounting, but still —"

Katherine gripped her mother's shoulders as the words sank in. "What do you mean, owning a computer-game company? Steve doesn't own anything — he tests computer games."

Grace peered at her oddly. "Well, he is CEO of HeartStar Productions. He must test the games his company produces."

"CEO? Of HeartStar?" Katherine's thoughts seemed to have scattered with the wind. "Steve Walker owns HeartStar?"

"Of course. He founded the company." Grace looked up at Katherine as if her daughter were certifiable. "He named it after Cora — Corazon Estrella is Spanish for HeartStar."

Katherine didn't blame her mother for thinking she'd gone around the bend; she felt pretty nutty herself. "How do you know all this?"

"Ralph told me, of course." She smiled impishly. "The man is a little eccentric, but you can't fault his pride in his son."

Katherine thought over the past several days. It was beginning to make sense — Steve's keen interest in computer games, the fooma bug for Cora's birthday, his vociferous defense of HeartStar. "I thought he was an overgrown teenager who played computer games all day."

"Oh, my." Grace's hand flew to cover her mouth, but a laugh escaped anyway. "So you thought you'd be safer with your dull-as-oatmeal accountant."

Katherine stared at her toes, feeling sullen as a child. "I thought you liked Alan."

Squeezing Katherine's arm comfortingly, Grace said gently, "He's all right. I'm sure he's a good provider. But I won't have you marry him if you don't love him, sweetheart."

As her mother's words penetrated, she felt the heaviness on her chest finally lift. The airy touch of joy that took its place whooshed inside Katherine, bursting out in laughter.

She threw her arms around her mother, tipping the witch's hat from Grace's head. "I shouldn't, Mama, should I? I shouldn't marry someone I don't love." Before she could pick up the hat again, the wind snagged it and started bouncing it toward the gym. Katherine retrieved it, then dashed back, and plunked it on her mother's head. "Thank you!"

Then she hiked up her skunk pants again and grabbed the tail to keep it out of the way as she ran. "Where are you going?" her mother called out after her.

Katherine danced around to face her mother. "To see Steve," she shouted over the sudden moan of the wind. Then she skipped across the yard, skunk tail held close to her body.

"It's okay to love him," she informed her heart, the softly spoken words catching on the wind. "He's a responsible guy after all, with a real job and a steady income."

She thrust aside the guilt she felt at how mercenary she sounded, even to herself. But she needed that security, damn it, after all those uncertain years with her father.

The spooky sounds emanating from the Haunted House drifted toward her as she neared Room 20. Dressed as twin Grim Reapers, Tim Hacket and Lindsay Horton, two of her brightest sixth-graders, stood guard at the entrance. They grinned and reached out for her as she approached.

"Here she is, Mr. Walker," Lindsay yelled to the dim figure lurking just inside the door. "Ms. Tipton's here."

About to call his name, she paused when a black-cloaked arm snaked out and beckoned her with a prompting finger. She wanted nothing more than to be alone with him just now, but she couldn't resist the invitation into his domain.

"Just wait, Ms. Tipton," Tim said as she

stepped over the threshold, “it’s *awesomely* scary.”

“Yeah,” Lindsay added, “only fourth-graders and above. Mr. Walker said the little kids would be too scared.”

A hand closed on each of her shoulders, and she craned her neck up, trying to see the face of who guided her. Although the fingers gripping her felt familiar, a death’s-head mask concealed the features of her sinister escort. A delicious chill coursed up her spine as the hands urged her between the folds of a black curtain into near darkness.

Something slapped against her and she leaped back as the raggedy thing suspended from the ceiling swung away from her. The thing spun and she saw the grotesque face of a stuffed effigy hanging from a noose. Its eyes wide, tongue protruding, it rocked and spun as she passed it.

“Yuck,” she muttered as Steve’s hands twisted her to the left. Something that felt like worms brushed against her face, and she squealed in horror. Scrubbing at her cheeks after she’d passed through, she shuddered, eyes straining to see what lay ahead.

A pleading whine sifted into her ears, accompanied by the groan of nails pulled from wood. A coffin lay at the next turn, illuminated by a pale green light. Bony fingers poked through the bare opening in the coffin lid, pushing against the hold of the nails. "Let me out!" the voice begged, pushing and clawing against the lid.

Past the coffin, what looked like hundreds of snakes writhed in a tank, and after that, an animated skeleton recited Shakespeare. A melting woman held court next to the skeleton, followed by a trio of ghostly musicians, all sixth-grade band members.

A rank rush of icy air, another black curtain, and she was out into the gusty October night air. Steve didn't follow her immediately; she waited, watching the curtain until he emerged without his mask and black robe.

Raking his fingers through his unruly hair, he grinned. "Have to keep up the illusion."

In his black turtleneck and jeans, he seemed real enough to Katherine. "Incredible," she breathed, although whether her praise was for the Haunted House or him she couldn't have said.

Just then a pop-eyed group of fifth-grade boys shuffled from the Haunted House exit. After a moment's silence, the knot of boys began to elbow each other and exclaim at the awesomeness of the Haunted House.

Steve placed a hand in the small of her back and eased her away. "Let's find a quieter spot."

He urged her into a dim alley between the school buildings where no one came and no one would see them. She turned and leaned up against the wall, her hands rising of their own accord to rest against his chest.

His hands covered hers, warming the chill from them. She looked away, then back at him. "I'm a little embarrassed."

His thumbs brushed the sides of her hands. "Why?"

His touch stole her breath, and it took her a moment to respond to his query. "My mother told me about HeartStar."

He laughed. "So you've realized I'm not the deadbeat you thought I was. You're not very observant sometimes, Katherine."

"You made very little effort to correct my erroneous conclusion," she scolded. "In fact, you may have deliberately misled me." Then she shook her head at her own denseness. "Good grief, CEO of HeartStar. Only the second biggest computer-game manufacturer in the state."

He gathered her hands between his, his warmth enfolding them. "And closing in on number one."

A burst of laughter echoed nearby, startling them from their intimacy. "Come," Steve said softly, pulling her deeper into darkness between the classrooms.

His hands cupped her shoulders, holding her loosely from him. "I've missed you," he murmured.

She could make out the shine in his eyes in the moonlight, but nothing more. "I've missed you, too," she whispered.

In the wind-swirled dark, there was only his heat, the restless sound of his breathing, a trace of seasonal woodsmoke mingling with his musky scent. Another sound — her own harsh breathing, rasping in her ears.

His fingers tightened on her shoulders, as if he intended to pull her toward him. Yet he hesitated.

It has to be me, she realized. *I have to make the first move.*

She could sense his tension in the dark and the limits of his barely held patience. She held power over him because he gave her that power when he gave her his love.

Overwhelmed by his gift of vulnerability, she felt tears prick her eyes and stepped into the circle of his arms. She curved hers around his waist, pulling him as close as she could.

The invitation was all he needed. Freed now by her willingness, his mouth dipped to hers, his tongue almost immediately thrusting inside. A long, low groan shook him as her tongue met his. She moved her hips more firmly against his, delighting in the hard evidence of his passion.

"Katherine," he gasped, the sound skittering away on a gust of wind. Her hands roamed across his back, caressing the firm muscle there, as she ached simply to draw him inside her. Impatient, she jerked the black knit of his turtleneck free of his jeans and with a sigh, traced her fingers across his bare flesh.

He was trembling, or she was; she couldn't tell. His mouth left hers, tongue trailing along her jaw, to the sensitive pulse of her throat. The tip of his tongue traced the shell of her ear, and her head lolled, shivers of sensation coursing through her body.

Her knees turned to butter, unable to hold her weight. He moved her back against the wall, then pinned her there with his body, his hips pressing against hers. His breath caught in his throat, and he gripped the sides of her head as if to hold himself back.

"We'd better stop," he said softly. "This isn't the time or place. No matter how much we want each other."

Katherine took a deep breath, unable to speak. She nodded slowly.

With what seemed an effort, he pulled away from her. She shivered with the sudden cold when his body left her. Lacing his fingers in hers, he guided her back into the moonlight, out of the temptation of the dark.

As they stood at the corner of the classroom, the wind caught her hair, blowing it across her face. Steve tucked the wayward strands behind her ear with infinite tenderness.

Katherine placed her palm against the back of his hand, holding it to her face. "I'm sorry," she told him. At his quizzical expression, she added, "I avoided you all week. I shouldn't have done that."

He shrugged, although she could see a hint of the hurt he'd felt. "I figured you needed some space."

She nodded, her free hand skimming across the silky knit of his turtleneck. "Have you?" he asked, gaze intent on her. "Come to terms?"

She nodded again, wanting to shout out "I love you," never mind who else heard. She opened her mouth, the words danced at the back of her throat.

The intensity of Steve's gaze strengthened, as if by sheer will he could pull the words from her. But she held back.

And she understood why. She had to talk to Alan first. Before she could declare her love for Steve, make that final commitment, she had to gently tell her almost-fiancé that she no longer intended to marry him.

Steve captured her chin in his palm. "What were you about to say?"

She rose on tiptoe to press a kiss to his warm cheek. "I'll tell you later."

As she backed away, she could see he was ready to argue. "Later," she vowed, running her fingertips along his jawline. "I promise."

"I shouldn't let this go," he growled as he turned his head to kiss her palm. "But when you touch me like that, I can't seem to hold two thoughts together in my brain."

She laughed, spinning away from him, her white-striped skunk tail swishing behind her. His brilliant smile, his bright eyes and their loving gaze held her entranced in the moonlight. She glanced quickly around her, then she pressed her lips to her palm and blew the kiss to him.

He snatched it from the air, pressed it to his heart, as he held her gaze for another long moment.

Then, her step as light as the cotton candy being twirled in the gym, she hurried back across the yard. *Tomorrow,* she thought, her heart brimming with joy. *I'll tell Alan tomorrow. Then I can go to Steve.*

As she stepped inside the gym, the loud welcoming warmth of the room enfolded her.

Steve watched Katherine go, the outrageous skunk's tail bouncing after her as she ran across the yard. He'd seen what he wanted to see in her eyes at last, the love she was finally letting herself feel.

As she disappeared into the gym, he whispered, "I love you," saying the words he knew had trembled on her lips. She'd refused to say them, but not out of denial. He was certain. She needed to tell Alan it was all over before she could come to him.

He spun on his heel to return to the Haunted House, whistling a decidedly un-Grim Reaper type tune. He fought a grin as he tugged on his mask and robe. First the EduSource deal, then the meltdown of Ms. Katherine Tipton. Of course, HeartStar's white knight purchase of EduSource, Inc. wouldn't mean much without Katherine's love. But at least the past week's negotiations with EduSource had given him something to think about besides broken hearts and erotic fantasies.

He'd give her a day, maybe two. Then he was buying a great big diamond ring and forcing the issue. Hell, he'd tell the accountant himself if he had to.

With his sinister mask concealing a cheerful grin, Steve turned to his next customer.

Chapter 9

Now that Katherine wanted so desperately to speak to him, why was Alan suddenly making himself scarce?

She set the receiver down gently before she gave in to the urge to snap it in two. That must have been, what? Call number ninety-nine. Ninety-nine times dialing Alan's number, ninety-nine repetitions of his voice intoning, "Please leave your name and number after the beep . . ." What the heck was he doing on a Sunday, anyway?

Katherine was wearing a rut in the rust-colored carpet of the flat. She should have called Alan last night after the Halloween carnival, never mind how late it had been. But since she hadn't wanted to drop the bomb over the phone, that would have meant a trip to his place at nearly midnight. And she'd been utterly exhausted after the school carnival.

She flicked a glance at her watch and swore. She was due downstairs ten minutes ago for Sunday dinner with Steve's family. She'd have to try calling Alan again later, or her talk with him would have to wait for another day.

When she hurried out of the autumn chill into the main house, the cozy camaraderie in the kitchen warmed her, clearing away her irritation. The twins peeled carrots at the sink while Corazon and Denny shared salad-making duties at the dining-room table.

"Where's your dad?" she asked Steve as he stirred a fragrant pot on the stove.

He took a sip of the rich brown stew, then added another shake of salt. "Out with your mom."

Katherine's eyes widened, then she laughed with delight. "I guess they really have hit it off."

"Yup," Steve said with a grin. Then he gazed at her sidelong, hand still stirring the stew pot. "Just like you and me," he said softly.

Katherine didn't pretend to misunderstand. "Right. If I'm the one you want."

He studied the brown, bubbling surface of the stew as if it carried the answers to the universe. He paused his stirring when the twins came over to drop handfuls of bright orange carrot circles into the pot. Then he waited until they were out of earshot.

"Don't you know that by now?" he asked quietly.

She pressed her fingers to his arm, the warm plaid flannel soft against her skin. "I think so," she assured him.

"What else do I have to do to convince you?"

"Keep kissing me. It's exactly what I need. Confuses me completely, you know."

Steve smiled at that as he dunked the carrots under the surface of the stew. "Melinda!" he barked in an excellent imitation of his father. "Slice the bread. Theresa, help Cora set the table."

"What can I do?" Katherine asked as the girls scurried out of the kitchen to their tasks.

"I'll let you help with the dishes after dinner," he told her, setting down the spoon and turning toward her. His warm hands curved around her neck, chasing away the last of the chill. "You wash," he murmured, placing a kiss on her left cheek, then her right, "and I'll dry," he finished, planting a third on her forehead.

Slowly, deliberately, he dipped his head down to her. His lips touched hers lightly, a bare tingle of sensation.

"First base," she whispered, and she heard the soft rumble of laughter deep in his throat. His tongue slipped inside, a teasing brush against hers. "Second," she gasped.

He angled his head to better advantage, and deepened the kiss, eliciting a sensual heat that suffused her body. *Home run,* she thought dreamily. *Slam-dunk. Goal!*

The sound of a clearing throat dragged her out of her languor. She looked up to see Cora, Melinda, Theresa, and Denny, wide-eyed and grinning, watching them.

Clutching at Steve to keep her knees from giving way, she grinned back at their curious audience.

"What are you looking at?" she asked pertly. She took the stack of bowls from Theresa's hands. Heat still rising in her cheeks, she turned to the stew pot and started filling them.

Katherine might have expected the third degree from Cora, or even the voluble twins, but everyone at the dinner table carefully avoided asking about "the kiss." Cora looked about to burst, her eager eyes looking from her father to Katherine and back again, but she held her tongue.

Later, as Katherine settled between the lumps in the mattress of the convertible sofa, she reflected how happy and excited

Cora had seemed about Daddy kissing her school principal. Of course, said school principal was pretty excited herself, after the most sensual dinner cleanup in history, followed by another knee-melting kiss in the garage apartment's living room. Katherine had been ready to say to heck with talking to Alan first, but Steve, gentleman that he was, had pulled away from her determined grip. Leaving her restlessly aching.

And her soon-to-be-no-longer-almost-fiancé still wasn't home. Katherine gave up calling him at midnight, slamming down the phone hard enough to cause a small crack in the mouthpiece. Well, she'd buy a replacement for Steve as a wedding gift.

A shiver trilled up her spine at the thought. Except for that remark he'd made about the two of them going up to Reno, Steve hadn't mentioned marriage. What if he only wanted a fling, an affair, a torrid tryst or two? She flopped impatiently to her other side, wincing at the jab of a convertible couch spring in her hip. She'd change his mind soon enough about that.

She grinned at herself in the darkness. Here she'd avoided setting a date with Alan all these months and now she planned to use everything short of a shotgun to herd Steve up the aisle.

Contorting her body into the one comfortable position between wads of mattress stuffing, she vowed to march into Alan's office first thing tomorrow morning. She'd notify Phyllis, the school secretary, that she might not be in until lunchtime, then beard the lion in his den. *Tomorrow,* she thought sleepily. *A clean break.*

Her eyes fluttered shut and she drifted off. Her dreams were vivid, full of shotguns and weddings and roaring lions.

Steve grinned at Marc Cohen, now former president of EduSource, and pumped the older man's hand. The three signed copies of the purchase agreement lay in neat stacks on the table in HeartStar's conference room. Signed, sealed, and delivered and it wasn't even 8 A.M. Monday morning.

"Sorry for the god-awful early call," Cohen said as he scooped up his copy of the contract, "but I'm due at the airport for a noon flight, and the wife insisted we settle the deal before our vacation."

Suppressing the urge to dance a jig, Steve escorted Cohen out of the conference room. "I hope you'll reconsider coming back on an advisory basis."

The man waved a hand in refusal. "My

wife would have my head. But I can recommend some people if you're still looking for an educational consultant."

"I think I've got that one handled," Steve said, as Cohen swung into his black Lincoln. "Have a great time in Europe."

Steve backed away, saluting the older man as he started his engine. Then when the Lincoln pulled out onto the street, Steve surrendered to his excitement and did a little two-step in the parking lot.

He had to call Katherine. She had to be the first to hear his news. As he hurried to his office, he glanced down at his watch. She was probably at school by now. He shut his office door and grabbed the phone.

A minute later, he set down the phone in disappointment. Katherine would be late this morning, the secretary had said. Calls to the flat and the main house yielded no clues to where she'd gone.

Then he remembered her unfinished business, the knot she had yet to untie. "Okay," he muttered, "I can be patient. I'll give her the morning." He dropped back in his office chair and glared at the phone, willing it to ring.

The clock hadn't quite ticked out ten minutes before he was on his feet and sprinting to the Mustang. He cranked the engine to a roar and backed, squealing, out of his parking space.

As he gunned out of the lot, he whipped Alan Linden's business card from his wallet and checked the address. To hell with patience. He was going to track her down.

Squirming in the driver's seat of her BMW, Katherine checked her watch again, then stared at the front door of Linden & Linden. Alan's beige sedan sat in its usual end slot, so she knew he was here. It was time she got off her duff and went inside.

She closed her fingers around the door handle and had to take a breath to still her shaking. Why in God's name was this so hard? She didn't look forward to hurting Alan, as her announcement surely would, but she knew he'd understand.

Then why did she feel as though she ought to be dragged from the car? *Because you're still afraid,* a little voice whispered. *Afraid you're risking a life like your mother's, with a will-o'-the-wisp like your father.*

But Steve isn't like Daddy, she reminded herself. HeartStar was an established, successful company, not a struggling, fly-by-night operation like the ones her father sank his money into. If Steve were like her father, he never could have built a company like HeartStar.

She shook aside her fears, her doubts. Setting her jaw, she pushed on the door handle and climbed out of the car. She smoothed her hands along her slim cream wool skirt, then snugged her turquoise-silk blouse more firmly in the waistband. She dithered over the cream jacket, then decided she'd have to manufacture her own courage, not cloak herself with it by putting on the jacket.

With trembling hands, she pulled open the glass door with its neat gold letters spelling out Linden & Linden. Ms. Beeker was absent from her post in the foyer, and Katherine nearly took that as her cue to escape. Giving herself an angry shake, she marched to Alan's door and pushed it open.

As she expected, she found her soon-to-be-ex-almost-fiancé behind his desk. Not so expected, his secretary was nestled comfortably in his lap.

Alan leaped to his feet, nearly dumping Ms. Beeker to the floor. "Katherine!" he shrieked, hastily straightening his mussed tie.

Katherine could only stare. Ms. Beeker

seemed caught between mortification and womanly pride that she'd snatched such a prize from Katherine's grasp.

Alan scraped back his hair with both hands as he rounded the desk. "I've been wanting to tell you, but I haven't had the courage."

Ms. Beeker preened a little, demurely settling her full skirt around her hips. With a shock, Katherine realized that some change had overcome Ms. Beeker, transforming her. Her hair seemed to positively shine, her stick-thin figure now seemed full of willowy grace.

A grin of recognition lit Katherine's face. "You two are in love, aren't you?"

Alan looked as wary as a feral cat. "Yes, we are," he said defensively.

A weight began to dissolve from Katherine's shoulders. "And you want to break off our engagement."

Suspicion still clouded Alan's face. "I've wanted to tell you for days now."

His behavior the day of the plumbing disaster popped into her mind. "That trip to Reno . . ."

He flushed to the roots of his pale blond hair. "There *was* a conference. It was all perfectly innocent. But Ms. Beeker and I —"

Still grinning like an idiot, Katherine approached the secretary. To her credit, she held her ground. Katherine asked her, "What *is* your first name?"

"Rachel," she said softly. "It's Rachel."

Katherine thrust out her hand, waited until the startled woman took it. "Congratulations, Rachel. I hope you two will be very happy."

Then she spun on her heel to go. "But Katherine!" Alan called after her.

Katherine turned back. "I'm very happy for you both." She headed for the door once more.

"Don't you want to talk?" Alan tried again.

"I do, Alan," Katherine tossed over her shoulder as she strode out of his office. "But you're not the one I need to talk to."

Katherine fidgeted at the front window in Steve's living room, staring outside as if by wishing she could conjure up the hot red muscle car. She knew he was on his way — his receptionist had just called, Cousin Denny told her when he let her in — but somehow, she thought she could bring him here faster by force of will.

Then the Mustang pulled into the driveway, and she almost wished he'd go away again. Her heart went ballistic, hammering in her chest, dancing with an equal mix of excitement, joy and dread. *He's here!* her heart sang. Then her stomach clenched in terror and squeaked out, *Good God, he's here!*

He seemed to fly from his car to the house, giving her no time to consider escape. He flung the front door open, then kicked it shut. Before she could as much as take a step toward him, she was folded in his arms.

His mouth covered hers, his lips moving almost with desperation, as if begging hers to open. She let him in willingly, trembling at the first touch of his tongue, reveling at the long low groan wrenched from him. He turned her, nudging her toward the sofa, then pulled her down into his lap. Unable to help herself, she squirmed against him, felt the impossibly hard ridge of him nestled against the center of her.

"Good God, Katherine," he groaned, "if you keep that up, I'm going to explode right here."

Heat rose in her cheeks at the implication of his words. She kissed him once more, then slid from his lap, drawing another groan from him. Once she was safely beside him, he pulled her close, tucking her head against his shoulder.

She snuggled her cheek against the smooth broadcloth of his shirt. "I talked to Alan," she told him.

He toyed with her hair, running the strands between his fingertips. "I was there right after you."

"Then I went looking for you." She touched his face as if he would disappear. "At HeartStar."

She heard the laughter rumble in his chest. "But I'd already left to look for you."

She pulled back a little so that she could see his face. "I have something to tell you," she whispered, eyes fixed on his.

"So do I," he murmured in response, "although I don't think my new venture excites me nearly as much as that light in your eyes."

He knew, she realized. She didn't even need to tell him. Her love for him shone in her gaze, danced in the very lines of her body. Overwhelmed by the joy of it, she leaned toward him again and pressed her lips to his. His mouth opened over hers, his tongue diving in, thrusting against hers until she thought her body would melt from the toes up.

With all the strength she could muster,

she pulled back again. Steve might know already, but she owed it to him to tell him straight out that she loved him. She parted her lips, took a breath to express all she held in her heart for him. Then what he'd just said began to seep in around the edges.

She stiffened in his arms. "New venture?"

He grinned, threaded his fingers into her hair. "I closed the deal on EduSource this morning. Remember that computer game I showed you the other night? I bought the company."

She scooted away from him so that his hands fell from hers. "You bought it?"

He seemed unaware of the chill that overcame her, so exuberant was he. "They're struggling. Hell, EduSource is this close to Chapter 11." He pinched off a bit of air between his fingers. "It'll be a challenge pulling them clear."

She tucked her arms tight around her middle, feeling her world crumble around her. "You bought a company that's nearly bankrupt?"

He finally recognized her distress. "EduSource has great potential. I can bring them around."

His words seemed to pound into her like

a Sierra winter wind whipping through the oaks. They echoed like her father's promises all those years ago. *It's a can't-lose proposition, Katie girl. This little company's going places. A surefire investment.*

"A surefire investment," she said aloud, her tone flat and cold.

He turned her toward him, confusion clouding his face. "No," he said slowly, "no investment is surefire. It's a risk — but it's a risk I'm willing to take."

She jolted to her feet, rapidly putting distance between them. She paced the room, struggling to remember where she'd put her purse. She found it finally by the door, fumbled in it for her keys.

Steve strode over to her, tried to take her into his arms again. She shrugged away from him. "Katherine, what is it?"

She closed her fingers around her keys. "You can take the risk, but I can't," she hissed.

He shook his head, as if grasping for understanding. "What are you talking about? What does this have to do with us?"

"Everything!" She groped for the front door handle, caught it on the second try. She swung the door open then rounded on him. "I thought I could count on you, Steve. Once I found out about HeartStar, I thought I could feel secure, that you wouldn't let me down. But —"

Her voice broke on a sob, and she hurried through the door. She would have slammed it behind her, but he got in the way. She raced to her car, shaking off his hand every time he would have reached for her.

She turned back to him once more just before she climbed into her car. He stood at the end of his walk, fists clenched.

"This has nothing to do with us, Katherine," he said between angry breaths.

Tell him now, her heart told her. *Take the risk.*

But she didn't, swinging inside the car instead, face forward to keep him out of her view. She pulled out quickly, catching sight of him in her rearview mirror before she turned off his street.

She wouldn't let herself cry at the image of Steve standing alone on the walk, watching her go. She refused to cry.

But her heart wept.

She called Phyllis from her house to let her know she felt ill and wouldn't be coming in at all. What had been intended as a lie became self-fulfilling prophecy when the press of tears behind her eyes made her head pound. Somehow, it seemed only what she deserved.

The house smelled musty, being shut up so long after the flood. She wandered from room to room, opening windows and the front and back door to let in the brisk October air. Still restless, she returned upstairs, stood hesitating in the hall when her eyes lit on the attic access.

She remembered a vague notion to clear out the attic clutter when the weather cooled and the space became more bearable. She supposed now was as good a time as any for a mindless task, something that might take the edge off the ache that overwhelmed her.

It took two leaps before she managed to grab the handle to the pull-down stairs. They groaned as she tugged them into position. She mounted the stairs without enthusiasm, wrinkling her nose at the attic's smell, even mustier than the rest of the house. She made a desultory effort to open the painted-shut window, then gave up.

In the cobweb-filtered light, she scanned the room. Boxes stretched across the cluttered wooden floor, the black marker notations on their tops and sides obscured by dust. Moving from box to box, she ran a trail through the dust with her fingertips, reading the markings on each one. Then her gaze roamed the room again, finally falling on a box snugged into the far corner of the attic, a small blue shoe box tied with string.

Her gaze stilled, resting on the small box. She crossed the room slowly, knowing what the box contained, afraid to look inside.

She picked it up anyway, carried it to the window. Seating herself on a sturdy cardboard carton, she untied the string.

"Oh, Daddy," she breathed at her first look at the contents.

There was the paper napkin from a restaurant in Oregon, folded into a flower. The broken sand dollar from a beach in Southern California she'd insisted she loved as much as a whole one, maybe even more. The necklace he'd made for her from gum wrappers, with its zigzaggy edge that always made her neck itch.

And the birthday cards. Not one for every year, of course, and most of what she had received had come late. But a fat stack of them, with cartoonish pictures of cowgirls or ballerinas on the front. They started at age three and continued until the last one at age fourteen.

The heart attack took him between her

fourteenth and fifteenth birthdays. The night they got the call still stood vivid in her mind — the phone ringing just after eleven that brought a sudden halt to the argument between her and Grace. The odd look on her mother's face even before she picked up the receiver. The tears pooling in her mother's eyes, spilling down her face as she spoke to the Nevada State Police. And the fact that he had died alone in a motel room, his dreams of wealth forever out of reach, wearing worn pajamas Katherine had given him when she was ten.

She swallowed back the memory, resisting the grip of tears. Putting aside the box, she began to examine the birthday cards, running fingers over the fuzzy embossing on the front of each one, reading the words, the age, then opening the card. Inside, the usual banal homily gave way to her father's hasty scrawl — *Love you, Katie* — then *Daddy* below that.

She flipped through to the last card. No cartoon figures on this one; it was her first real grown-up card. A simple vase of flowers adorned the front, the blues and soft corals faded with time. *To a loved daughter,* it said on the front, and inside, the usual impersonal verse.

But in this card, penned in neater letters below the printed lines, as if he'd taken exquisite care with the words, her father had written a verse of his own. *To Katherine,* it said, followed by five simple lines.

You've brought me riches
Far beyond what any man could hope for,
Wealth a man could never spend.
I love you more than I can tell you
More than you will ever know.

Her hands shook, and one wet tear fell to swirl away the "y" in Daddy. She set the cards aside and buried her face in her hands. Finally, she let herself go, her sobs loud and painful, washing away regrets and could-have-beens, leaving behind a clear, clean space.

He'd loved her. Her father had loved her. He'd let himself be hazed by dreams sometimes, but near the end, he'd understood that his true wealth lay in her, in her love. Finally, finally, she could let down the bitter barrier between her heart and his love. She could believe again as she had as a child, that she was precious to him.

She was still wiping away the moisture in her eyes when she heard the scrape of footsteps on the attic stairs. Even before

Steve's head appeared above the attic floor her heart began to sing, feather-light as it now was. When he hesitated halfway up the stairs, she felt too tear-weary to rise, instead letting the joy in her face bring him to her.

He hurried up the last few steps and across to her in seconds. Pulling her to her feet, he covered her face with kisses. Then he centered his efforts on her mouth, thrusting possessively with his tongue, teasing hers into dueling with his. She clutched at his shoulders, grasping at his realness, endlessly grateful that he'd followed her here.

Finally he pulled back, his eyes fierce. "I won't let you shut me out."

She shook her head. "I won't shut you out."

He locked his fingers behind her neck, holding her head still. "We'll talk about this, work through the problems."

"Work through the problems," she repeated, her eyes on the corners of his mouth, wanting to taste him there.

"I can't back out of the EduSource deal," he continued, "but I can assign someone else . . ."

His voice trailed off. His eyes fixed on the motion of her tongue as it stroked her lower lip. Humor warred with arousal in his face. "If you keep doing that, I'll forget the rest of my speech."

She raised her eyes to his, lost herself in their fire. "Sorry," she said, tracing his jawline with her fingertip. "Maybe you could just cut to the chase."

His smile widened into a grin. "Marry me," he said.

"Yes," she responded.

"I love you," he told her, with almost a warning in his tone.

"And I love you," she said back, her heart in her words.

He laughed, exultant. Then he pulled her into an embrace so tight the breath exploded from her lungs. She held on to him for dear life, reveling in the feel of his hard chest under her hands.

"I love you, Katherine Elizabeth Tipton," he murmured, brushing his lips against hers.

The bare contact demoralized her more than the deeper kiss had. Her breath came out in a long sigh and her hands moved restlessly across his chest, fingers seeking out the buttons of his dress shirt.

Steve chuckled, a forced sound, then captured her hands. "I want you so badly I could explode," he said roughly. "But I guess I'm old-fashioned enough to want to make it official first."

Her fingers struggled free to drift back down the placket of his shirt. "Then let's go to Reno," she murmured, slipping a button free. "Now."

He snagged her hands again, thwarting her attempt to dip inside and skim his chest. "My father would have kittens if he couldn't go to my wedding. I'm sure your mother would feel the same."

Katherine sneaked past his guard and pressed a kiss against the bare triangle of flesh she'd laid bare. Then she tipped her head back. "She'll want to run things," she warned. "She'll have us setting a date six months from now."

"No way." He shook his head. "We leave for Reno tonight."

"I'm holding you to that," she said, then took his hand and tugged him toward the attic stairs. He gave her a toe-curling kiss just before they descended, then another at the bottom. When she sat at the edge of her bed and picked up the phone, he snuggled next to her. She had to dial her mother three times because his teasing touch caused her fingers to stumble over the buttons.

"Not home," Katherine told him, when

her mother's answering machine picked up. She brushed a kiss across his lips, acutely aware of the bed that stretched out behind them.

He pulled her to her feet. "I can't sit at the edge of temptation and hope to resist. Let's go tell my dad."

Another kiss before he gunned the red Mustang's engine, several more at each stop sign along the way to his house, another in the driveway. He captured her in a particularly soul-melting sensual embrace on the front porch, then he pushed the door open.

Once inside, Steve kicked the door shut. The two people on the sofa sat up straight. Katherine just gaped at them.

"Mother!" Katherine exclaimed and her mother popped to her feet like a Grace-in-the-box, tugging out of Ralph's arms.

Grace's hands blurred in a flurry of movement, buttoning and tucking, although she missed one waving collar tip that brushed her ear. "Katherine," she said sedately, her dignity marred somewhat by her disheveled hair.

Less self-conscious, Ralph rose and flung an arm around Grace's shoulders. When Katherine might have expected her mother to shrug out of the embrace, she snuggled closer with a shy smile.

"We want you two to be the first to know," Ralph said, giving Grace a squeeze. "We're getting hitched."

Katherine's shock quickly gave way to jubilation, and she ran to throw her arms around her mother. Steve did the same to his father.

"You might have beat us to the announcement," Steve told Ralph as he squeezed him in a bear hug, "but you won't to the wedding. Unless you'd like to go to Reno tonight to make it a double."

Grace gasped and pulled back from Katherine's embrace. "You and Steve?" When Katherine nodded, her mother screamed out a very unladylike whoop of joy, then gave Katherine a hug that would have made a boa constrictor proud.

"I love you, Katherine Elizabeth," her mother said, the words choked with tears.

"I love you too, Mom," Katherine responded. Then her eyes rose to meet Steve's over her mother's shoulder. The words "I love you" passed between them, the message born in their eyes — and in their hearts.

Epilogue

Katherine snuggled more tightly against her husband of eight months despite the end-of-June heat simmering in their bedroom. She skimmed her palm across Steve's bare chest, tracing a path through the sandy dusting of hair there. His skin was still damp from their shower, and its coolness soothed her palm.

The fan blades above them cast inadequate puffs of sultry night air against her naked body. "My mother would get married on the hottest day of the year," Katherine groaned.

"That's the downside of a June wedding," Steve said as he nuzzled in her hair.

Katherine turned to give him better access, at the same time wrapping her leg around one of his. "Do you think your father will ever forgive me for selling him my house?"

His seeking lips brushed along her throat to her jawline. "You didn't know the water heater was about to give out."

"And the roof."

"And the furnace," he added as he drew gentle teeth over her earlobe. "He loves it.

He's never happier than when he's fixing up a house."

A shiver coursed through her as his tongue teased the shell of her ear, the sensation as fresh and intense as the first time he'd touched her. She would never tire of his lovemaking. Each time, he found something new to bring into it, sometimes tender, sometimes sensual, sometimes downright outrageous.

His hand trailed down to curve against one soft breast. "Are you sorry you resigned from Gardenview Elementary?"

She propped herself on one elbow so that she could look at him. "I told you," she said, tapping a scolding finger on his chest, "that I will miss the kids, and the staff, but I won't miss the problems."

"You'll have a new set of problems as the EduSource educational consultant," Steve reminded her.

"Nothing I haven't already had to handle part-time," she said, tucking herself back beside him. "And that while holding a full-time job."

He resumed his exploration of her body, stroking the creamy underside of her breast. "I just wondered if you regret your decision."

She heaved an impatient sigh. "First, I

love my new job at EduSource. Second, Cora has four more years at Gardenview. I'm sure I'll have my fill of the place by the time she graduates sixth grade." She shifted so that she lay atop him. "And third . . ." she said softly.

"And third?" he managed as she settled herself over the now-hard ridge of him.

"And third," she purred, "if you don't make love to me right now, I'm asking Cousin Denny for some of that aphrodisiac he's been testing."

"If you make me any hotter for you than I already am," he growled as he turned her under him, "you'll need a fire extinguisher."

She laughed with delight, then the laughter melted into a moan as his lips and hands caressed her. She responded in kind, with flesh against flesh and whispered words of passion.

And their bright love flared, illuminating the night with joy.